Lord Knole was certainly full of surprises. Priscilla had seen little of Englishmen's fashions, but she did realize that his snowy white unmentionables and his dark blue coat fit him well. The coat set on well-proportioned shoulders and the unmentionables molded to sinewy thighs. She glanced up into his face to see him frowning.

"Miss Springton," he began carefully, "a lady really should not look at a man's, er—"

"Legs?" she suggested when he seemed at a loss for words.

He froze. "You shouldn't even acknowledge that a man has legs."

A puzzled frown touched her brow. She had seen plenty of bare male limbs in India. The field workers would have passed out from the heat if they had not dressed for the climate. "Everyone has legs," she said matter-of-factly.

"Yes, but you are not to mention them."

"Really?" What a strange country she had come to live in.

Also by Rebecca Ashley:

A SUITABLE ARRANGEMENT *
A LADY'S LAMENT *
LADY FAIR

Published by Fawcett Books

THE RIGHT SUITOR

Rebecca Ashley

FAWCETT CREST · NEW YORK

A Fawcett Crest Book
Published by Ballantine Books
Copyright © 1989 by Lois Walker

Library of Congress Catalog Card Number: 88-91294

ISBN 0-449-21547-4

Manufactured in the United States of America

First Edition: February 1989

Chapter 1

"It's so wonderful to be back in England!" Priscilla's mother exclaimed.

Priscilla glanced from her mother, who was seated across from her in the elegant crested carriage, toward the window. The green, rolling fields and overabundance of trees looked strange and unwelcoming to her. "It's not at all like India," she murmured, and wished for the thousandth time that she were back there.

"Heavens no! We shan't have the dreadful heat or the dust." Her mother leaned across to pat Priscilla's cheek. "Don't look so unhappy, dear. You will like it here."

Priscilla wondered. She had spent the last seventeen years of her life, from the time she was five years old, in another country. To her, England was a foreign land.

The carriage swayed to a halt, and a moment later a dark-skinned servant opened the door. Priscilla stepped out into a courtyard that fronted a grand house.

"This is your home, dear." Her mother beamed.

Priscilla looked at the cold, forbidding house and ached to be back in India.

Her father, a stout, balding man, walked up beside her. "Beautiful, is it not? There is a two-story entrance hall beyond that screen of stone pillars. See all the windows in the upper floors? There will be good light in all the rooms."

Priscilla thought of the low, airy home with keyhole arches that she had left behind and felt a lump rise in her throat. She forced herself to say, "It's very grand, Papa."

"Indeed it is. Come along inside."

She followed obediently, listening while her father proudly explained the elaborate chimneypiece of plaster strapwork in the entrance hall. She remembered playing around a much more modest fireplace before they had moved to India.

Her father paused in the midst of an explanation of the cornice-stone. "You look confused, child. Is anything wrong?"

"I know I was very young when we left England, but I remember a much smaller house."

Her father flushed and coughed. "There was, er, another house before. But this is where we live now," he finished heartily. "You shall grow quite fond of it."

With those words ringing in her ears, Priscilla followed a servant upstairs to a lavish green-and-gold room that was to be her bedroom. All the family's possessions had been shipped ahead of time, so her brightly colored gowns already hung in the wardrobe. Even with the addition of her clothes and her personal set of ivory combs sitting atop the cherry-wood bureau, she felt displaced and unhappy.

Her gaze fell on the easel and brushes by the window and some of the knot went out of her stomach. At least she had her painting to help her endure a

2

season in London among strangers. But how was she going to adapt to being the wife of an Englishman? She knew little of the English and even less of men.

In India, her family had lived in a remote part of the country, far from Bombay and Calcutta where her fellow countrymen resided. Priscilla would have been content to live out her life there painting and riding and reading the books she ordered through the mail. But her parents had insisted it was time to return to England. It was, they said, time for her to marry Lord Knole.

Two days after the Springtons arrived in Kent, Lord Knole came to call.

He was dressed impeccably in a bottle-green waistcoat that was almost the same shade as his eyes. If there was so much as a speck of lint on his coat, it was more than his valet had been able to discern. The earl's cravat was tied into the intricate and crisply perfect Mathematical. If anything was less than perfect about Lord Knole at that moment, it was the frown on his handsome features as he tapped on the front door with the head of his brass cane.

Springton's letter had come as a surprise. Naturally, the earl had eventually meant to make the journey to welcome his old overseer back to England. But Springton had written obliquely of urgent business to be discussed. The earl could not imagine what sort of business. What was more, the note had come when Lord Knole could least spare the time. But he felt obliged to go. After all, he owed Springton a favor.

The door opened and Lord Knole found himself staring at a dark-skinned servant dressed in a robe and turban. Good heavens, Springton had actually brought their servants from India to this remote part of Kent. What in heaven's name had the man been thinking?

"I'm here to see Mr. Springton," the earl said in response to the man's silent look of inquiry.

"Sahib is in the library. Follow please."

The earl followed the small man down a hall newly carpeted with a Persian runner. The smell of fresh paint hung in the air. The servant opened a pair of French doors and stepped aside, bowing out of sight. Lord Knole walked into a study crowded with old leather books, gigantic porcelain urns and antique jade vases. He glanced up into the gaping mouth of an elephant's head and instinctively backed up.

"Knole! Good to see you." A man sprang up from behind a cluttered desk and came around to pump his hand enthusiastically. "You're looking demned fit."

"Thank you," he said with quiet dignity. "I hope you are well."

"Splendid! Care for a cheroot?" The stout older man pushed a box in his direction.

"No, thank you."

Springton lit a cheroot for himself.

"I trust your family is well rested after your journey?" Lord Knole inquired politely.

"I'm the picture of health. And of course my daughter is. She's never sick, you'll be pleased to know."

The earl let that odd comment pass.

For the next few minutes they exchanged polite information about weather and mutual acquaintances. Lord Knole, not having been offered a chair, remained standing. In addition, the smoke was starting to burn his eyes. He decided to speed the visit along by directing the conversation to the matter at hand. "You said in your letter that you had some business you wished to discuss with me."

"Ah, yes." Springton puffed cheerfully, tapped ashes into the brick fireplace, and propped an arm back against the mantle. "You no doubt remember my daughter."

The earl nodded. He had a vague notion of a dark-haired child playing around her father's office years ago when Springton was overseer for one of the Knole estates.

"She is two-and-twenty now and ready to be presented."

The earl blinked. The chit was too old to make her debut. Besides, Victor Springton was a nabob. He had gone to India and made money in trade, but he did not have a place in society. Knole's own association with Springton was a tenuous one based on the fact that Springton had once saved Knole's father's life. For that the earl was grateful. It was the reason he had taken such pains to respond to Springton's singularly unusual summons.

Abruptly, the older man jumped up and walked to the door. "I want you to meet my daughter." Without waiting for a reply, he shouted down the hall. "Priscilla! Come here."

A moment later a young woman appeared in the doorway. She was wearing a powdered wig of the type the earl had not seen since he was a young boy. Her dress was a heavy gold brocade that harkened back to his grandmother's days.

To give her credit, even with heavily powdered cheeks, some natural glow showed through. Her eyes were a becoming shade of blue, and the bones

5

of her face looked dainty beneath the enormous white wig.

Her father beamed proudly. "This is my daughter, Priscilla."

The earl executed a bow over the stiff hand she offered. "I am most pleased to meet you, Miss Springton."

"It is an honor, a pleasure, and a privilege that I should make your most noble acquaintance, milord," she said in the most stilted bit of phrasing he had heard in some time.

He maintained a pleasant smile. "It must be good to be back in England after all these years."

She hesitated, then said carefully, "I'm sure I shall grow to like it."

What a strange chit. He thought she would be overjoyed to escape from a life among savages to the civilized shores of her homeland.

"She's settling in very well," her father said heartily. "Go along now, child. Lord Knole and I have matters to discuss."

She dropped a low curtsy. "Good day, milord."

As the door closed behind her, Springton turned to the earl. "Pretty gel, what?"

"Charming," he lied.

Springton hesitated. "And most anxious to be wed. Truth to tell, I am not sure how to draw up the papers. You have only to tell me what you consider a suitable dowry for Priscilla, and it is yours. I am sure you know I made a deal of money in India. She is my only child, and I wish to see her married well and wanting for nothing."

"I understand how a father would want the best for his child," the earl murmured tactfully. As long as he wasn't the bridegroom, he added silently. Surely he had misunderstood Springton.

"I think you will make a fine husband."

The earl bit back a sigh, no longer able to ignore the direction of the conversation. "You want me to marry your daughter?" More than a few women had thrown themselves at his head since the death of his wife seven years ago. Oddly enough, he had determined to choose a wife this very Season. But if and when he did, it would be someone ideally suited to the position. Priscilla Springton, with her odd manner and outdated clothes, was definitely not that woman.

"I am sure you will be excellent for her. Don't be alarmed by how delicate she looks. She's stronger than she appears. I've no doubt she will bear many fine, healthy children."

Lord Knole's thoughts went to Margaret, who had died in childbirth with their son. Sweet, shy Margaret. She had been the ideal wife; he doubted anyone else could come close, certainly not Springton's daughter. He cleared his throat, and continued carefully. "Mr. Springton—"

"Call me Victor."

"Victor. I do not wish to be ungrateful, and I deeply appreciate the honor you do me. Priscilla is a lovely girl. However—"

"You needn't ask her to marry you right now," Victor interrupted. "You will have plenty of opportunity during the Season to do that."

Ah, yes, the Season. Springton had mentioned it earlier. He wondered if the older man understood that one needed connections to launch a daughter. "Do you have entrée into society?" he asked bluntly.

The older man's face wrinkled into a puzzled frown. "Entrée?"

"Yes. You must know the right people and have

the right connections to receive invitations to the parties and routs and particularly to the rooms at Almack's."

Springton was unperturbed. "Surely you can see that we are invited. You must know people in London."

Lord Knole knew everyone who mattered in fashionable London, and he was accepted everywhere. Springton, however, was another matter. Having made his money in trade, he was not likely to gain admittance into the select circle of the *ton.* "Mr. Springton, quite frankly, I don't believe that I can help you."

The older man blinked. "Is it because there are three of us? Mrs. Springton and I need not go up to London just yet. Take Priscilla on up and introduce her to a few people. You've the right of it. Three people might be difficult, but it won't be hard to manage an invitation for just one more person."

The man really hadn't the least notion of how things were done, the earl realized with a repressed sigh. He could not escort an unmarried woman about town without exciting comment. She must be properly chaperoned at all times. And who would agree to undertake the task for such an ill-prepared chit? Especially one of her advanced age?

"Or marry her here and forget about London entirely," Springton offered.

"I shall make arrangements for your daughter to come to London. I think it the least I can do for you to help see that she is presented." Looking the older man squarely in the eye, the earl continued, "I am honored that you would consider me worthy of your daughter, but I must tell you plainly I cannot accept the honor."

The older man frowned. "Why not? She's a pretty

gel, and she is possessed of a fortune." His voice rose as he waxed persuasively. "I made more money in India than you can possibly conceive of. Why, at this very moment, I have enough to buy—"

"Mr. Springton, money is not the issue."

The older man ground to an astonished halt. "Not the issue? Of course it is. With enough money a man can buy anything."

"Not a bridegroom. There are other factors involved in that. As an earl, I must consider my station when selecting a wife. I need someone trained in the management of a household and someone who is eminently acceptable in society." He tactfully let that sink in. "I will, however, undertake to see that she is presented properly. London abounds with men who would be very suitable marriage partners for your daughter."

Mr. Springton looked befuddled, but he nodded.

"Now then," the earl continued briskly, "as soon as I return to London, I shall begin making arrangements for her. I shall notify you when I am ready to have her sent up."

While her future was being planned, Priscilla paced her room. She wished she did not have to marry the earl. She was accustomed to dark-eyed, black-haired men, and the earl's blond hair and green eyes made him all the more an enigma. To her he represented a world about which she knew nothing and had little desire to learn. Especially if it involved such silliness as wearing this ridiculous wig. She pulled the offending item from her head and let her own dark curls tumble down. Using a linen handkerchief, she scrubbed the powder from her face until her cheeks bloomed with color.

Then she faced herself defiantly in the cheval glass. Slowly her shoulders sagged. She must marry

Lord Knole. Mama and Papa had talked of little else for the past months, and she could not disappoint them. And if she must wed, one man was as good as another.

By the time Lord Knole arrived back in London, he had had ample time to reflect on his promise to Victor Springton. And to regret it. Who was he going to find to supervise the entrance into society of a girl who had nothing to recommend her?

Genteel widows and impoverished countesses often undertook such a task for a fee, but they expected the girl to have the proper accomplishments. The earl suspected Springton's daughter had none of the necessary social skills. Where would she have acquired them? Springton himself had been an overseer and his wife a baker's daughter.

Perhaps, the earl reflected as his carriage headed into the elegant confines of St. James Square, he could find some nobleman desperate for funds, and a marriage could be arranged without Priscilla ever having to come to London. That would save everyone a deal of trouble and inconvenience.

Lord Knole settled back against the squabs, resolving to make some discreet inquiries at White's. There must be dozens of men who would accept any bride as long as her dowry was large enough.

In a day or so, he would look into the matter.

What he had no way of knowing was that Priscilla was already on her way to London. Victor Springton, always impetuous, had ignored the earl's parting words that he should wait for word of when to send Priscilla. Why couldn't she go up now? Victor Springton had asked himself. There seemed no reason to wait. After all, the Season was going to start shortly, and he didn't wish it to begin without his daughter present.

So Priscilla left for London the morning after the earl departed.

Sitting in the grand carriage, she was restless and apprehensive and fidgeted accordingly. She tried to pass the time by speaking to her maid, Maria, in Maria's native tongue and by looking out the window. But it was difficult to concentrate on conversation or on the scenery when she was so miserable. She didn't wish to go up to London, and she didn't want to marry the earl.

Papa had been very encouraging when she left. "The earl is anxious for you to go to London. Don't be nervous, child. He'll make you a fine husband. He only wants a bit of getting used to."

Priscilla thought that all of England and the people in it were going to take getting used to. In the inn where she spent the night, she lay awake into the wee hours of the morning and fervently wished that she were back in India.

The closer she got to London, the greater were her reservations.

As the carriage rolled into the city, she turned to her Indian maid. "I don't know why I must enter English society when I care nothing about it. And I don't like being here by myself." It had come as a shock to learn that her mother and father were not accompanying her. She was close to her parents. The family had always been together in India, and she felt uneasy going to a strange city in a new land alone.

Looking out the window at the narrow, crowded streets, the maid tried for optimism. "There will be many things to paint here."

"Yes," Priscilla agreed. But her heart felt heavy

11

when the coach stopped in front of a white marble house lined with Ionic pillars. She alighted in front of the mansion and walked with resignation up to the door.

A starched butler answered her ring.

"I'm Priscilla Springton. I've come to see Lord Knole," she said.

"He's out at the moment. Would you care to leave a card?"

She shook her head. "No. I've come to stay. Please show us to our rooms."

The butler's mouth fell open. He stared first at her and then beyond her to the elaborate carriage and the dusky-skinned maid. "Perhaps you have mistaken your direction. You are certain it is Lord Knole whom you wish to see?"

"Yes."

He cast another uncertain look about and pulled nervously at his collar. "And your name again?"

"Priscilla Springton. My father is Victor Springton," she added.

It was a name that had carried weight in India, but the butler only looked at her blankly, hesitated, then said, "Please follow me to the drawing room."

Priscilla walked into the marble hall and stared up at the twin staircases sweeping up each side of the room. The house looked cold and formal—the way the earl himself had seemed.

"This way, please," the butler prompted.

She followed him beneath the heart-shaped opening made by the staircases and into a room with severe brown draperies hanging from arched windows.

"I shall send for Lord Knole," he said and withdrew looking somewhat distracted.

Priscilla would rather have gone to her room and rested but she supposed it must be considered proper for her host to greet her before she did so. It was hard to know what was expected of her among these foreigners. In India she would have known exactly what to do. Her father had been a great friend of many of the Indian princes.

To take her mind off her present situation, she walked over to a painting of peasants at a fair and began to examine it. It was beautifully done with brush strokes so clever she had difficulty distinguishing them. Bending near, she examined the perfection of a woman's outstretched hand.

Priscilla was absorbed in studying the technique of the painting when the front door opened. She heard quiet, muffled words followed by footsteps. Then Lord Knole stalked into the drawing room and stared at her.

She dropped a low curtsy. Why was he frowning at her so darkly? "I was admiring the painting," she said when the silence seemed excessive.

"What are you doing here?" he demanded tightly.

She stiffened. In India a guest, even a complete stranger, was made to feel welcome. Her chin went up. "I've come for the Season." As well he should know. *He* had invited her.

After a long pause, he cleared his throat. In a somewhat gentler tone, he said, "Miss Springton, I fear there has been a misunderstanding. You cannot stay in the home of an unwed gentleman without a chaperone."

"I have my maid."

He dismissed that with an impatient wave of his hand. "That is not sufficient."

"Then what am I to do?"

"A good question," he muttered. "Well, you are

here now, so there's not much to be done about it."
Without another word, he turned on his heel and
stalked out of the room. "Rowles, show my guest to
suitable rooms."

"Yes, milord."

"I shall stay at the club. Have my clothes sent
over. And my valet, of course."

"Very good."

Priscilla stood in the drawing room, blinking in
amazement. The earl had treated her as if she were
an intruder instead of his future bride. Were the
English always so excitable and disorganized? She
had somewhere gained the impression the nobility
was given to cool serenity. She hoped once she and
Lord Knole were married, she would be able to
make him a calmer man.

Chapter 2

Shortly after the earl left, a petite maid appeared, introduced herself briskly as Esther, and took Priscilla upstairs to a room with somber striped wallpaper. The furniture was gleaming mahogany and the large bed was covered with a dark canopy. Priscilla thought again of the spacious, cheery rooms she had known in India.

"I will have a bath prepared for you," Esther announced crisply.

Priscilla's own maid had been led away to the servants' quarters shortly after their arrival. Maria had looked apprehensive; Priscilla understood the feeling.

Taking off her bonnet and pelisse, she laid them on the bed. She was brushing the dust from her skirts when a male servant appeared carrying a copper tub. Two women trailed after him with pails of steaming water. The bathtub was placed on the glazed delft tile in front of the fireplace and filled with water.

The servants departed, and then the English maid began helping her undress. Priscilla was not overly modest, but she was accustomed to her own maid. Here in this new household, among people with strange accents, she felt odd taking off her clothes.

She would get used to it, she promised herself as she eased into the hot water. She had no choice but to get used to it, did she?

An hour later, clean from her bath and wearing a bright red cotton gown she had bought in Calcutta, Priscilla sat on a stool by the window while Esther dressed her hair. The door opened, and a pretty, brown-haired woman entered.

"Miss Springton? I'm Lady Roseman. I'm married to Lord Knole's cousin. The earl asked me to look in on you while he makes arrangements for you."

How strange that the earl had not made arrangements before her arrival, Priscilla reflected. But Mama's parting words had been to be kind and charitable and to give her fellow countrymen the benefit of the doubt. She was trying.

Lady Roseman ran a critical eye over Priscilla's red dress, smiled sweetly, and asked, "Do you have other clothes?"

"Of course." She had a trunkful that had been made specially for her in India. Mama had hired a native seamstress who had copied from the yellowed fashion plates Mama had secured somewhere. Priscilla had exact duplicates of the gowns that had been worn to the coronation of King George II.

"Excellent. Quite honestly, dear, red is inappropriate for a young woman who has not been presented."

"Oh." Red was one of her favorites. But she consoled herself that she still had a pretty bright yellow and a bold blue she could wear. Lady Roseman's gown, Priscilla noted, was pale green and of a style

16

she had not seen before. The neckline was low and scooped and the waist began just below her ladyship's bosom. There had been nothing like this in the fashion plates of the Coronation of George II. "Your gown is unusual," she said politely.

Lady Roseman smiled. "Do you like it? It's an Empire style. They're all the rage."

Priscilla frowned. "All the rage? What does that mean?"

"In style. Fashionable," the other woman translated.

Priscilla was puzzled. Mama had told her that fashion at court never changed.

"Well," Lady Roseman said with a cheerful smile, "since you are settling in well enough, I shall let you finish dressing." Quick humor flickered in her eyes. "I think you have made things very lively for the earl."

Uncertain what to say, Priscilla murmured, "Thank you."

After the door closed, Esther continued silently styling her hair. When the task was completed, Priscilla's dark curls were swept atop her head and secured with dainty ivory combs. Little tendrils of hair framed her heart-shaped face and danced around her ears.

She had never worn her hair this way, but she liked it. It seemed a pity to cover it with that dreadful wig. "Is it proper to go without my wig?"

The maid pursed her lips. "Most definitely."

Priscilla smiled her relief. The wig was heavy and hot. She knew she must wear it to parties, but if she didn't have to wear it inside the earl's house, so much the better.

"What gown do you wish to wear tonight?" the petite maid asked.

17

Priscilla selected a heavily beaded orange silk with a huge full skirt. The maid seemed to hesitate, then wordlessly helped her into it.

An hour later, Priscilla walked into the elegant cream-and-crimson dining room. The earl was already seated at the head of a long, linen-draped table.

She dropped a low curtsy to him. "I hope the evening finds you well, Lord Knole."

He glanced at her from behind flickering candles. "You needn't bow like that," he said curtly. "I'm not the Prince Regent. No, don't sit there. Come sit near me so we don't have to shout down the table at each other."

"Yes, milord." It was an effort to keep her voice pleasant.

A footman pulled out the chair and she sat to the earl's right. Once she was seated, he made no attempt to speak to her. She bit back a sigh of irritation. It was all very well for Mama to suggest being charitable, but Mama was not having to deal with the earl.

"Lady Roseman came to see me," she said by way of conversation.

"Hmmm." Lord Knole didn't even glance at her.

Was he always so absorbed in his own thoughts? she wondered. Priscilla was glad for the diversion when the servants began placing dishes in front of her.

Dinner consisted of a whole array of food she had never tasted before. She politely sampled each of the dishes and smiled her approval to her host. He did not return a smile. When he looked at her at all, it was with an expression of distraction, as if he were trying to think his way through a problem.

At length he said abruptly, "This is a deuced

awkward situation. Quite plainly, getting you into Almack's is hopeless. I could try speaking with Sally Jersey, but things being what they are . . ." He let the words trail off.

Confused, she waited.

"The viceroy's ball is tomorrow. I daresay I could take you as my guest. There will be dancing and a light supper at midnight. You *do* know how to dance, don't you?"

Affronted, she lifted her chin. "Of course."

"Good."

"Mama taught me the minuet," she added with dignity.

He stared for a full minute. Then he cleared his throat. "I have been given to understand the British in India stay current with dances and fashions. What dances were the other English in India doing?" he demanded.

"I would not know. We didn't live around many English. Only missionaries and miners."

"Missionaries and miners," he repeated faintly. "The Season begins next week. I could not find a dancing master to teach you on such short notice even if it were possible for you to learn that quickly." He shook his head. "It is truly hopeless. The best course for everyone is for you to return to Kent."

Priscilla brightened. If all the English were like the earl, the Season would be a long and difficult ordeal. She jumped at the chance to escape it. "I can leave tomorrow," she offered eagerly.

"I think you should."

After that, the earl grew more relaxed, even unbending enough to offer her a glass of claret at the end of the meal.

"I've never tasted it before," Priscilla confided with a shy smile.

He filled her glass. "No time like the present."

She sampled the sweet drink. "Mmmm. It's good."

He picked up the crystal decanter and refilled her glass. "Here, have another. It's a night for celebrating."

She finished the second glass and smiled at him. He was becoming more appealing. She was even beginning to like his fair hair and green eyes. "Could I have a bit more?"

He laughed. It was the first time she had heard the earl laugh, and she found it a surprisingly pleasant sound—deep and sonorous. Something intriguing twinkled in his eyes, sending a warm flush over her. "I think not," he said. "You'll need a clear head tomorrow for the journey back." Rising, he came around to the back of her chair and pulled it out for her.

Regretfully, she set her glass down and rose. "Goodnight, milord." She took a step and was surprised to find herself wobbling. Immediately a strong, steadying hand was on her elbow.

"I'm fine," she assured the earl.

He didn't let go. "I'll walk you to the stairs."

"It must have been the roast beef," she murmured.

"Of course."

Priscilla couldn't be certain but she thought she heard suppressed laughter in his voice.

At the stairs, she took hold of the banister and turned to give him a grave nod. "Good night, milord."

"Good night." The smile was still there.

She smiled back at him and started up the steps.

Priscilla didn't mind that she had to concentrate on where she placed each step as she made her way up the stairs to her room. She was too happy about the thought of leaving in the morning.

Of course she knew she would have to marry the earl eventually, but she had been given a reprieve from the Season. In her present frame of mind being married to Lord Knole did not even seem such an unpleasant thing. One of the last things Papa had said to her before leaving was not to be discouraged if the earl at times did not act like a proper bridegroom because he *did* wish to marry her. In the later part of the evening, Lord Knole had almost seemed like someone she could enjoy.

Mostly her thoughts, however, were centered on her joy at being able to return to Kent.

Guilt is a terrible thing, Lord Knole decided as he sat that night in a brocade wing chair. He was in the paneled room of his club, an unread newspaper crumpled in front of him. If he sent Priscilla Springton back to her parents, he was effectively sentencing her to a life on the shelf. The only chance she had of finding a husband was in London. She would not be able to make a brilliant match, but there must be an impoverished nobleman who needed her dowry.

Naturally, the earl could never get her into Almack's, but if she attended a few of the smaller functions as his guest, he might find her a mate. Then he would have repaid his debt to Springton.

The girl must have more social graces than he had yet seen. She had surely met *some* cultured English people in India, in spite of what she had said earlier this evening. With a little time, he hoped she would acquire enough polish to capture a down-on-his-luck viscount or a baronet whose requirements for a wife were not so particular.

She would have to learn how to dress if she was to attract any man. An outfit like she had worn to dinner would scare even the most desperate suitor away. Her hair had looked better than when he first met her, he was glad to note. At least she had not been wearing that outlandish wig. Lady Roseman could offer her excellent advice on fashion. With a little work, the chit could be brought up to snuff.

Satisfied with that conclusion, the earl closed the paper and went up to bed.

The sun was rising when Priscilla awoke the next morning. Birds tweeted a welcome song.

Swinging jauntily out of bed, she crossed the soft Aubusson carpet to the window. A sapling in the large, brick-enclosed garden swayed gracefully in the breeze. It promised to be a beautiful day for the trip back. Maria had packed the trunks late last night. She had seemed as eager to leave as Priscilla. As soon as they had breakfast and thanked Lord Knole, they could be on their way.

The door opened behind her and the Indian maid entered.

Priscilla had known Maria since both were thirteen. The Indian woman seldom said much, but it was still a comfort to Priscilla to be with someone she had known in India. It was even more of a comfort to be leaving London.

Maria stood quietly, awaiting instructions.

With a stroke of daring, Priscilla said, "Instead of wearing one of those cumbersome English frocks, I shall wear the striped muslin." It was a flowing, unrestricted gown of the kind the native Indian women wore. It would be comfortable for traveling.

22

Since she was making the trip home alone, she decided it would do no harm to dress for comfort rather than style.

Maria unpacked the gown and helped Priscilla dress. Then Priscilla went downstairs to wait in the library for the earl.

An hour passed and still he did not return from his club. It was almost eight in the morning. Where in the world could he be? When Priscilla put that question to a maid who appeared in the library with dust-cloth in hand, the plump woman stared at her.

"Begging your pardon, miss, but it's very early. I don't imagine his lordship will return for four or five more hours."

Four or five hours! Priscilla's spirits fell. How was she to amuse herself for that length of time? She was far too restless to read a book, even if she had had any idea where the library was in this huge house.

After fifteen minutes of pacing aimlessly, she went upstairs and unpacked her easel and paints. Then she returned with them to the picture she had admired yesterday in the drawing room. The scene looked even more compelling upon second inspection. She was bending close to study intricate details when a servant found her and insisted on fetching a lamp and tall stool for her.

Thus comfortably arranged, Priscilla began to paint in earnest. As she busied herself duplicating the large picture on her own small canvas, she forgot her impatience to be away. She was thoroughly engrossed in her work when the door opened and Lord Knole entered.

She glanced toward him, and he actually smiled at her.

"Good morning," he said.

23

She jumped down from the stool and started to drop a low curtsy. Remembering herself, she drew up sharply and murmured a polite greeting.

He pulled his greatcoat off his shoulders and handed it to the little valet who had followed him in. "Why don't we adjourn to the breakfast room, Miss Springton? We can talk there."

Talk? He must mean say good-bye, Priscilla decided as she left her painting equipment on the stool and followed him down the hall to a room with ornate moldings around the ceiling and a black marble fireplace. Food in warming plates was laid out on the sideboard. A servant filled a plate for each of them and quietly departed.

Priscilla sat next to the earl at the oval table and pointed to her plate. "What are those?"

He looked startled. "Kippers. Surely you've tasted them before?"

"No. We didn't have them in India." She sampled one. Not bad, she decided, and tried another one.

"I have been giving your situation some thought," the earl began gravely. "Since you have come all this distance to London, it seems a pity for you to turn around and go back to Kent."

A quiver of unease shot through her. "I don't mind," she assured him quickly.

Lord Knole continued as if she had not spoken. "That being the case, I think it would be proper for you to attend some of the smaller functions with me."

"You mean I'm not going back to Kent?" Disappointment hit her with the weight of an anvil.

"Not at present." His glance fell on her dress for the first time, and he frowned. "I shall send a messenger to Lady Roseman asking for her help in selecting some more fashionable gowns for you. We must not impose on her overmuch but, under the circumstances, I am sure she will assist."

Priscilla was more intent on persuading him she should return to Kent than wondering what the "circumstances" were. "Yesterday we decided it would be best if I went home," she reminded him, trying not to sound plaintive.

"That was yesterday," he said patiently.

"What has changed since then?"

He sighed. "Miss Springton, pray do not be obstinate. You have not fulfilled your mission for coming to London. It would not speak well of my gratitude to your father if you were to return unattached."

Her argument died under his quelling look.

"There is a soiree tonight," he continued. "I suspect that some people who once lived in India will be present. I had intended to go to the viceroy's ball, but perhaps this would be better for you. I am persuaded you would feel more comfortable at the soiree."

Stifling her disappointment, she grasped at the only positive thing she could see in the situation. He said there would be people from India present. She would be glad to see them. Perhaps she would even see someone she knew. She had been fascinated by the maharajas and their families. Did the men bring their harems to London? she wondered. She had always been curious about those doe-eyed women behind veils.

The earl rose. "Good, then it's settled."

There was actually kindness in his smile. They were curious people, these English, Priscilla decided. Lord Knole was certainly full of surprises. She had seen little of Englishmen's fashion, but she did realize that his snowy white unmentionables and dark blue coat fit him well. The coat set on well-proportioned shoulders, and the unmentionables molded to sinewy thighs. She glanced up into his face to see him frowning.

"Miss Springton," he began carefully, "a lady really should not look at a man's, er—"

"Legs?" she suggested when he seemed at a loss for words.

He froze. "You shouldn't even acknowledge that a man *has* legs."

A puzzled frown touched her brow. She had seen plenty of bare male limbs in India. The field workers would have passed out from the heat if they had not dressed for the climate. "Everyone has legs," she said matter-of-factly.

"Yes, but you are not to mention them."

"Really?" What a strange country she had come to live in.

"No, you must not," he repeated firmly, and strode from the room.

Priscilla fought back the impulse to make a face after him.

She was unable to return to her painting for very long. Lady Roseman arrived a short time later. Her gaze swept over Priscilla, and her smile faltered.

"Dear me. I had thought we might go out shopping, but you simply cannot be seen out in that. Well," the other woman continued briskly, "I've brought fashion plates. We can select styles from them and pick out the fabric later."

Regretfully, Priscilla put down her brushes. "As you wish."

The two women sat down side by side on the Chippendale sofa. Lady Roseman flipped through the pages. "Too old. Too young. A bit overdone. *Très chic* but not for someone as slender as you."

Priscilla blinked at the bewildering array of pictures. None of them looked at all like the fashion plates from which her dresses had been made.

Lady Roseman stopped. "This one would be perfect for you."

The gown in the picture was cut low enough to reveal some bosom. Priscilla shook her head firmly. "I couldn't wear that."

The dark-haired woman turned to her. "Whyever not?"

"It's not modest."

"Well, it's not as demure as some gowns, but it certainly isn't indecent. It's appropriate for someone being presented but still tantalizing enough to attract a man's notice."

Priscilla was silent. It was all very puzzling. Only this morning the earl had lectured her on modesty. Now it appeared that certain transgressions were acceptable and others not. She would never, she was sure, learn the ways of the British.

Lady Roseman selected two other gowns, then closed the book. I'll have some of my clothes sent round for you. They may be large but they'll do until something can be made. Besides, you'll need something to wear this evening."

"I have a trunkful of my own clothes," Priscilla pointed out.

Her ladyship patted Priscilla's hand. "Trust me, I know what I'm about. Let me see, you'll also need fans and gloves and calling cards and a thousand other things." She ticked the items off on her fingers. "What a lot to manage. But, a Season is well worth it."

"They don't have Seasons in India," Priscilla

noted wistfully. "Except hunting seasons," she amended. "But killing a tiger is not the same sort of thing, I daresay. It's much more bloody."

Lady Roseman looked horrified. "Priscilla, dear, it will not do for you to talk this way in front of other people. A young lady being presented should confine her conversation to talking about her finishing school, her musical accomplishments, and her love of children."

Priscilla thought it threatened to be a very long evening at the soiree.

Priscilla and Lord Knole arrived at the soiree at nine o'clock. Lady Roseman was attending a ball elsewhere, but had loaned Priscilla a green satin gown that fitted perfectly over her slender hips. Her dark hair was pinned back with ivory combs, also loaned by Lady Roseman. Her ladyship had donated a beautiful white lace shawl along with some parting advice, "Smile and say as little as possible."

Priscilla stepped into a salon that appeared modest after the grandeur of the earl's house. She glanced quickly around at the people present but saw no Indians. They must be arriving later, she decided.

Lord Knole kept a proprietary hand on her arm as he escorted her toward an aged couple. "Miss Springton, this is Mr. Reynolds and his wife," he said formally.

The short man and wife scarcely looked at her. Their attention was all for the earl. They beamed at him.

Priscilla started to drop a curtsy, but the earl held her upright by strengthening his grip on her arm.

Smiling politely, she said, "I'm very pleased to meet you."

"Miss Springton is the guest whom I sent word I would be bringing," he explained.

The hostess and host's attention remained fixed on him. They looked awed, as if unable to believe their good fortune at his presence.

Dinner was announced almost immediately, and the dozen people present adjourned to a small dining room.

"Lord Knole, you sit here," Mrs. Reynolds chirped, motioning toward the head of the table.

The earl hesitated near the place marked with Priscilla's namecard at the foot of the rectangular table. Reluctantly, he released her arm.

Priscilla had not realized that she was clinging so tightly to him until she was left to stand on her own. Forcing a smile, she sat in the chair he pulled out for her. She tried not to feel bereft when he walked away. He might not be her friend, but he was the only person present that she knew.

The elderly woman seated next to her smiled faintly and murmured, "So you have lived in India?"

"Yes."

"The Indians seem to me to be a most peculiar race."

Nerves made Priscilla talkative. "Actually, there are many races. There are Telugu Brahmins. They are the ones who are short of stature. The Pathans are taller and less pigmented. In the South, of course, are the Kadar and Pullayan—" She broke off. Was she boring her listener? "I should let the Indians explain the differences when they arrive."

Her neighbor's voice rose in astonishment. "We are expecting Indians tonight?"

Several people looked toward the two women. Priscilla flushed.

Lord Knole smiled urbanely. "I suggested there might be some people coming who have spent time in India. They are British, of course," he continued, as if it were absurd ever to have had any doubt on that head. He turned pointedly to the man beside him. "Tell me, Sir Joshua, how is the hunting on your property this year?"

Chatter resumed around the table. Priscilla sat rigidly, feeling foolish and awkward. If this was a taste of what society life was like, then she was going to dislike it even more than she had imagined. She harbored no kind thoughts toward the earl either. He had looked at her as if she were a troublesome child.

She wished she could leave. People around her continued to talk, and an occasional smile was directed at her, but no one engaged her in direct conversation.

It seemed an interminable time before the evening was over. The moment they entered the carriage, she tossed her shawl haughtily up onto her shoulder and announced to the earl, "I do not wish to attend any more parties. I had a perfectly dreadful time tonight." Reflecting on her evening, tears welled up in her eyes. She pushed them back with determined blinks.

Perhaps he sensed her unhappiness, for his voice was gentle. "I daresay it was unpleasant. The next party won't be as bad."

"I will not go to a next one." She spoke defiantly, hoping he didn't see her chin tremble. "I think we should get married immediately and return to the country."

"So Springton didn't believe me," he muttered.

30

His sigh was followed by a long silence. Finally, he said gruffly, "There will be no marriage between you and me."

Her lips parted in astonishment. "But Papa said—"

"I know what your father told you, but that is not the case. I had hoped to find a suitable man for you during the Season."

She looked at him in the uneven light from the coach lanterns and saw the determined line of his jaw.

Amazingly, she felt hurt. She did not want to marry the earl, but the realization that *he* did not want to marry her cut at her pride. "Then I shall return to Kent," she said flatly.

"You would be well-advised to give that decision some consideration. If I understand correctly, your parents returned to England from India in order that you might wed. They will be sorely disappointed if you do not. Eventually you would regret your impetuousness. Every woman needs a husband, and I owe it to your father to find one for you."

Chapter 3

She could go home, Priscilla told herself that night as Maria helped her undress. She could return to Kent and tell her parents that the earl was a dreadful man. That was precisely what she ought to do.

She repeated the thought to herself later as she thumped at her pillow and restlessly sought a comfortable place on the bed. She had already endured an unpleasant evening at the soiree. The fact that the earl was not going to marry her put a cap on it.

Well, she didn't have to stay in London. She could leave.

Priscilla sat up, irritably freeing her legs from the covers she had somehow managed to wrap around them. The wind from the open window caught at her hair and blew it back behind her. Even the wind felt different than it did in India, she reflected with a surge of sadness. Why had her family ever left there?

For her sake, she reminded herself. All the elaborate plans to return to England had been made with a view to her future marriage. How would her parents react if she went back to Kent and said she did not wish to wed? Sighing, she realized that her father, never one to accept defeat easily, would probably bring her right back to London. He was, alas, entirely capable of ignoring the earl's stated disinterest in her and embarrassing her by insisting that Lord Knole marry her. *That* she could not endure. It had been bad enough to hear the earl tell her that he had no desire to marry her.

Lying back on the bed, she acknowledged unhappily that she had little choice except to stay and try to find another husband.

A bitter smile caught at her lips. What a ridiculous position to be in. She, who had no wish for any man, was now going to have to make herself smiling and accommodating to some somber Englishman who probably didn't know a Brahman from a Bengal tiger.

The next morning, swallowing her hurt pride, she prepared herself to convey that message to the earl. Over breakfast in the brick-enclosed garden, she sat across from Lord Knole at a small table. The sun streamed down through a large lime tree, and yellow primroses growing nearby perfumed the air.

Conversation between the earl and herself thus far had consisted of terse greetings.

"I have decided to remain in London," she said stiffly.

He nodded disinterestedly. "I shall endeavor to find someone to groom you for society."

"Very well." They subsided into silence. Priscilla wished she could tell him she had never wanted to marry him. It was humiliating that he had said as much to her. Her only satisfaction was in the fact that no other woman wanted to be wed to him, else why was he still unattached? Finally, curiosity over how long she could expect to remain in London overcame her dislike for the earl, and she asked, "Is it difficult to find a husband?"

He frowned. "Miss Springton, you really should not ask such a question of me. Certainly you must not ask it in polite society."

She pushed aside her almost full plate. "Why?"

"Because when a lady comes to London, she comes to be presented. Finding a mate may be her *real* objective, but it is considered unacceptable to speak of it in such bald terms."

She stared at him. This was clearly another case like that of legs—something that existed but was not to be discussed. Why could the English not say what they meant and be done with it? "I shall never remember all the silly rules for your society," she said crossly.

He straightened his broad shoulders. "They are not silly. They are what well-bred people abide by, and you must abide by them as well. Furthermore, when I find someone willing to launch you, I expect you to work very hard to learn the finer points of civilization."

Deep down inside Priscilla felt rebellious, but she was too cowed by his cold stare to show it. She suspected that even men flinched under that unyielding gaze. Looking at him now, it was difficult to believe he had ever shown any warmth, however slight, toward her.

"Do you understand?" he demanded.

"Yes, I do." She wished her voice didn't sound so soft and insignificant.

However, it seemed to mollify him. In a more amenable tone, he continued, "I realize that last night was unpleasant for you. Once you know the ways of English society, you will find the soirees more to your liking."

"I hope so," she said honestly.

For some reason that amused him. "Spending a

Season in London is not the worst fate that could befall you, you know."

"No, I suppose I could be set upon by tigers."

He threw back his head and laughed. "There, you see." Still chuckling, he pushed back his chair and rose. "And now I shall do my utmost to find you a chaperone."

She watched him go, puzzled by her own conflicting feelings. She was used to dealing with many different kinds of people. In India she had met Muslims, Christians, Buddhists and Sikhs. But she had never known anyone quite like the earl. Just when she had firmly made up her mind he was thoroughly unlikable, he would smile or laugh. And then she became confused.

Mrs. Speers was short, fat, and nearsighted. She had a white lace handkerchief tucked into the bosom of her gown, and her lips were a bright red. She spoke with her hands waving and some sort of an accent Priscilla found difficult to understand.

She was Priscilla's new chaperone.

Lord Knole, Mrs. Speers, and Priscilla were standing in a small parlor in the older woman's home. The room showed signs of having been hastily cleaned. A box of chocolates peeked out from beneath the Hepplewhite sofa. A feather boa was tucked behind a chair cushion. Priscilla suspected that the straightening had taken place while she and the earl had waited in the hall with the maid, and Mrs. Speers had caroled out to them, "I shall be out momentarily."

Mrs. Speers smiled fondly at Priscilla. "I think we shall deal extremely well together, Christina, dear."

"It's Priscilla," the earl corrected.

The aging woman smiled. "As the bard said, 'A rose by any other name would smell as sweet.'" Forefinger laid across her lips, she circled Priscilla. "A lovely child. Good bone structure."

The earl nodded disinterestedly and glanced toward the door.

"She doesn't yet carry herself with majesty, but she will when I am finished with her."

"She does not need to be able to pass for a princess," the earl said crisply. "The important thing is that she learn to conduct herself well in polite company."

Priscilla bit back the tart remark that she did not yet feel she had *been* in polite company. Instead, she confined herself to mutely studying the paintings on the wall. None were of the superior skill of those in Lord Knole's house—a fact she hated herself for noticing.

"Leave everything to me, milord." Mrs. Speers's red lips parted in a cheerful smile. "I fancy I know something about young ladies." She patted Priscilla's cheek.

"Very well. I must be on my way." Turning to Priscilla, he said, "Your trunks will be delivered this afternoon. If you need anything, you have only to send word to me."

"We will be perfectly fine," Mrs. Speers assured him gaily.

With one final, doubtful look around the room, he took his leave.

"Now then," Mrs. Speers said briskly, "we may as well start immediately. I have some improving books I wish you to read." She crossed to a cluttered bookcase, pulled out several volumes, and handed one to Priscilla.

She looked at the cover. "*The Maiden Is Abducted*?" she said doubtfully.

"Oh, I meant to give you a very nice one on deportment." Mrs. Speers took the book back and flipped through it. "Dear me, it says, 'He carried her up to his bedroom in the dark and gloomy castle and shut the door behind them. She struggled in his arms but his greater strength prevented her from freeing herself. Alone with the wicked man she could only cry out for mercy.' Hmmm."

Such a book as this had once arrived by mistake in a shipment from England, but Mama had not allowed Priscilla to read it. Now she leaned over to finish the page. Mrs. Speers continued reading to herself, her lips moving silently.

"What a dilemma for the poor child," Mrs. Speers murmured. "Let us sit down and see what she is to do now."

They settled themselves side by side on the blue striped Hepplewhite sofa. Mrs. Speers pulled out the chocolates.

"Have one, dear."

Priscilla accepted.

Together they ate and read.

Gradually day wore into evening, and the light faded. Even though she was guiltily aware that Mama would not approve, Priscilla still did not abandon the novel. In fact, she became so engrossed in it that she scarcely glanced up when the maid came and lit the candles.

Throughout the reading, Mrs. Speers cried, laughed, offered advice to the heroine, and paused from time to time to deliver moral lessons to Priscilla. "She should not have left her home against her parents' wishes." "She should have known by the dark look in Percival's eyes that he meant her no good."

Priscilla agreed.

Both women turned to each other with a sigh when the book ended well for the maiden.

Mrs. Speers rose. "Tomorrow, pet, we shall start dancing lessons. You shall be as graceful as a swan by the time I have finished with you." She started to leave, then paused, frowning. "Have you been shown to your room?"

"No."

"We must find you a place to sleep," Mrs. Speers announced vaguely, and departed.

Left alone, Priscilla wondered if she would be forgotten. She liked her chaperone but suspected her of absentmindedness. She had seen the same behavior in a Hindu woman who had served in their household in India.

However, a bedraggled maid arrived after a time and showed Priscilla to a second floor room. It was small compared to the earl's grand accommodations, and there were dust balls in the corners. All the same, she went to bed feeling at ease for the first time since her arrival in London. It might be tedious to learn the ways of the English, but she would work very hard at it. Because once she had mastered the rules, she would be able to marry and quit this awful town forever.

With that thought in mind, she fell asleep.

Priscilla slept late the following morning. It was almost seven when she awoke. With Maria's help, she dressed in the blue gown Lady Roseman had loaned her and went downstairs eager for her lessons to begin. Unfortunately, Mrs. Speers proved to be a late riser. By nine o'clock, restlessness drove Priscilla back upstairs to find her paints. Then she set about copying a picture in the dining room. The picture of three women at a well was obviously a copy itself, but the lines were good and she set about her task enthusiastically.

Mrs. Speers appeared shortly after noon. The red on the older woman's mouth strayed outside the bounds of her lips, and the color on her cheeks looked suspiciously unnatural. A froth of lace handkerchief blossomed at the neckline of her low-cut gown. She sat down at the table.

"Good morning, pet."

Priscilla was almost certain Mrs. Speers had forgotten her name, but she couldn't think of a tactful way to remind her, so she contented herself with a simple, "Good morning."

"I had the most dreadful dreams last night. I was locked in a castle by an evil man." She opened a drawer behind her and pulled out a box of chocolates. "I'm far too distressed to teach anything today. We shall rest and enjoy ourselves and tomorrow we shall begin our lessons." Oblivious to Priscilla's look of surprise and disappointment, she popped a chocolate into her mouth and licked her fingers. "Tell me what South Africa was like."

"India," Priscilla corrected.

"Are you certain it was not South Africa?"

"No, it was India. I lived there from the time I was five years old."

"I'm sure you have a thousand tales to tell about it. . . ."

"Oh, yes," Priscilla said eagerly. "I've ridden elephants and—"

"However, you must not speak to men of dangerous situations and exciting countries that they have not seen. Far better for *you* to be entertained by *their* tales of adventures. Therefore, we shan't speak of India."

Priscilla subsided back in her chair.

"Ladies talk about gowns, hairstyles and the weather."

"That's all?" Priscilla asked plaintively.

Mrs. Speers smiled slyly. "Well, there are also *on-dits* to be discussed."

"*On-dits*? I don't know that word."

The older woman looked startled. "It's the latest gossip, of course. You poor lamb, you know so little. Well, never fear, you will learn soon enough."

"I'm sure she will, my dear aunt," a male voice interjected.

Both women looked up to see a man with black hair lounging in the doorway. He was dressed in a brown waistcoat and ivory pantaloons. He twirled a gold watch in his right hand.

"It's my nephew Geoffrey," Mrs. Speers explained to Priscilla, quite as if he were not present. Turning to him, she said, "Geoffrey, do come in and meet Miss Springdale."

"Springton," she murmured.

"Yes, yes, of course. It's Miss Springton, Geoffrey."

He bowed over her hand, blowing a kiss on her knuckles. "Charmed, Miss Springton."

"It is an honor, and a privilege, and a pleasure to make your acquaintance." Priscilla didn't find the newcomer handsome, but he was dark-haired and brown-eyed, and that was reassuringly familiar. Judging from the way he was studying her, he found her novel as well.

He settled himself in a chair and smiled at her. "You have not been in England long, I apprehend?"

"Only a short time."

"She is being presented this year. Lord Knole asked me to undertake her presentation. I was fortunate enough to be available," Mrs. Speers added importantly.

One eyebrow went up at the mention of Lord Knole. Geoffrey turned back to her. "He is your guardian?"

Priscilla could tell he was impressed. "My father is Victor Springton," she said, wanting to let him know that her family was important in their own right. Papa's name had always invoked respect in India. Yet Geoffrey only shrugged. "I've not heard the name. Are you connected to the earl through his wife?"

"The earl's wife?" Priscilla repeated. *What* wife?

"Poor Margaret," Mrs. Speers put in. "She was so sweet. And such a lady. Everyone said theirs was the perfect match."

"She died," Geoffrey interjected.

"Such a lovely woman and such impeccable lineage." Mrs. Speers dabbed melodramatically at her eyes. "She died in childbirth several years ago. I nothing doubt his heart was broken, which is why he has never remarried. But, of course, he must remarry eventually. The heir, you know."

"I didn't know," Priscilla murmured. The sweetly romantic story tugged at a chord in her heart.

"Pardon me, ladies, but we seem to have strayed from the subject. Miss Springton was explaining to me how she is connected to the earl."

"My father once worked for Lord Knole as his overseer," Priscilla said.

Conversation came to an abrupt standstill. Geoffrey stared at her. Mrs. Speers fluttered her hands nervously. "You must never say that, pet."

Priscilla turned a puzzled gaze on her. "But it's true." And it had not made any difference to the people in India. There Papa had gained respect on his own merits by hiring Indian workers in his mill and treating them fairly.

"It doesn't signify," Mrs. Speers said with further distracted waving of her hands. "Tell anyone who asks that the families are connected. Be vague. But whatever you do, never tell the truth in London."

"Unless it makes you look better than you are," Geoffrey added dryly.

Priscilla felt suddenly close to tears. It was too complicated. And to think she was enduring all this in order to find a husband—something she didn't even want. If only she could go back home to India and the peaceful life she had known there.

Mrs. Speers pulled the handkerchief from her bosom and offered it to Priscilla. "Don't look so cast into the doldrums, pet. You shall have a splendid time during your Season. It is only in the beginning that things may be a bit difficult. But you're pretty, and I nothing doubt you will take."

She resolutely blinked back tears. "Take?" she asked in a small voice. "I don't know what that means."

"Why, it means that men will vie for your attention. You won't end up on the shelf. Don't you agree, Geoffrey?"

He looked her over critically. "Yes, I think men will find her most interesting."

"See there. And you have such a lovely figure. In nice, new clothes, you will stand out to advantage."

Priscilla nodded miserably. But she was glad when Geoffrey left, and Mrs. Speers departed shortly afterward to attend to business of her own.

Left alone, she again immersed herself in her painting.

It was a long time later before she went up to her room. Maria was there unpacking her clothes. She seemed to be moving slowly and without enthusiasm.

"I hope you are not too disappointed that we shall not be returning to Kent," Priscilla said.

Maria made no reply.

"We won't have to remain in London long." Only until Priscilla found a husband.

Maria nodded gravely. "Yes, miss."

"Even when we leave London, though, we shall remain in England. I miss India," she added pensively. "I am persuaded that you must, too."

"It will pass," Maria said softly.

"Yes," Priscilla agreed, and hoped that it passed quickly.

"You entrusted her to Mrs. Speers! Robert, how could you?"

"I had precious little choice. How many women do you think I had to ask before I even found her?"

Lady Roseman subsided back onto the sofa across from the earl. "I suspect it was several. I wish I could help you more with the child, but I won't be able to go out in public at all shortly. My confinement, you know."

Lady Roseman was the wife of Lord Knole's favorite cousin. The couple had been married six years, and her ladyship had yet to produce an heir. Now that she was enceinte, she was taking great care to insure that all went smoothly.

"I shall keep as close an eye as I can on her progress. All this comes at a deuced bad time. I have estate business to attend to, and I have other things

43

on my mind." Most specifically, he meant to find a wife.

"It may not take long to find someone for her," Lady Roseman consoled him. "She has a sweet smile. In the right clothes and hairstyle, I think she could be enchanting."

"All she has to be is passable," Lord Knole muttered. "I don't expect her to bring London to its knees. I simply want her off my hands."

That same thought was in his mind that afternoon when the earl arrived at Mrs. Speers's house. He alighted from his curricle and walked toward the modest house prepared to do his duty, but wishing to dispense with it quickly.

A footman in new green livery greeted him at the door. He was a new addition to the household since the earl's last call. Lord Knole suspected he had been hired with Mrs. Speers's newfound wealth. Having correctly deduced that he was desperate for someone to launch Priscilla, Mrs. Speers had not come cheaply.

The earl handed the dapper footman his beaver hat and walking stick. "Kindly tell Mrs. Speers that Lord Knole is here." He heard the sound of piano music coming from the nearby drawing room. "On second thought, I'll announce myself."

"Very good, sir."

As he suspected, dancing lessons were in progress. The earl stood in the doorway and watched unnoticed while a wizened man played the piano. Mrs. Speers watched from the side of the room. In the center of the room, Priscilla struggled with the steps of the boulanger.

"No, dear," Mrs. Speers admonished, "not such long strides. Short and dainty. And hold your head up proudly."

Priscilla was wearing a new, pale blue gown in the current fashion. Her hair had been cut shorter, allowing curls to play about her face. Lady Roseman had been right: the chit was pretty. Certainly, she was comely enough to attract a second glance from men.

Priscilla looked over and spied him. Color rose in her cheeks, and she stumbled to a halt. "Good day, milord."

"Good day, Miss Springton." He tried for a friendly tone. "How go the dance lessons?"

"Splendidly," Mrs. Speers lied brightly.

Priscilla said nothing, but her face was lined with unhappiness. Drat the chit; he was doing the best he could for her. Yet he felt guilty knowing this was so difficult for her.

"Some of the country dances may be more to your liking," he offered.

"Perhaps," she agreed without conviction.

"She shall love them," Mrs. Speers chirped.

The earl turned toward her. "Could I beg your indulgence in allowing me to speak to Miss Springton alone a moment?"

"Certainly!" Mrs. Speers addressed herself loudly to the deaf piano player. "Edgar, let us leave Lord Knole and Miss Springton to chat." She whisked the elderly pianist out of the room, discreetly leaving the door open behind her.

The earl walked toward Priscilla. "Do you have everything you need here?"

"Yes." She didn't meet his gaze.

"Do you like it here?"

She shrugged and moved her toe along the border of the carpet.

Only the fact that he was a consummate gentleman kept him from taking her by her slender shoulders and shaking her. Could she not see that he was trying to look after her welfare?

"Tomorrow I shall take you for a drive in the park." He was not sure what had prompted him to make that offer. Her disinterested expression strengthened his doubt. "Everyone of consequence is seen riding along Rotten Row," he informed her stiffly.

"Indeed."

"I shall call for you at one o'clock." Head lifted proudly, he stalked out of the room. The girl didn't even have the sense to know when she was being done a favor. Dozens of women would give a great deal to be in her place.

He hoped she did find a husband quickly. He didn't relish the thought of dealing with her any longer than was absolutely necessary. She had a stubborn, defiant streak that he would never tolerate in a wife. In fact, Priscilla Springton had altogether too much spirit. Some of that would have to be taken out of her if she was to find a husband.

Chapter 4

"It's a dashed fine likeness of the original," Geoffrey marveled.

"Do you really think so?" Priscilla was pleased beyond reason at his compliments. In the short two weeks she had been at Mrs. Speers's house, she had already made copies of three paintings. Except for the maid who was forced to dust around her, no one had seemed to take much note of her work or her talent. Until today. Geoffrey had stopped to visit his aunt and happened upon Priscilla where she was working in the parlor. He had been lavish in his praise.

Standing by the mullioned windows, eyes squinting critically, he turned the painting this way and that. "Amazing. It is identical to the original. You really do have a gift."

"Thank you," she murmured, coloring prettily.

"Have you done any others?"

"I have two more in my room," she confided.

"I should like to see them. I am persuaded they are as exceptional as this."

"You're too kind." She felt shy and proud at the same time.

"And you, my dear, are too modest. These should be displayed, not hidden away in your room."

"It's only a copy," she murmured. But she was not opposed to hearing more compliments. In fact, she was prepared to discuss her work all day. It was simply that no one had seemed the least bit interested until now. Geoffrey's praise made her generous. "Would you like to keep the picture?"

His eyes widened in surprise. "I should like it above all things."

"Then it is yours." She smiled at him. Until now, she had been uncertain about how she felt about Mrs. Speers's nephew. At times he had seemed arrogant, and she had once heard the maids gossiping that he gambled heavily. But now she liked him extremely well.

"I shall have it framed for you," she said.

"That's quite unnecessary. I have the perfect frame at home for it." He looked directly into her eyes. "I am pleased beyond words that you have given it to me."

Priscilla was still radiant two hours later when the earl called to take her for a drive in Hyde Park. She had been driving once before with him. Mrs. Speers had told her he was taking her to increase her "consequence" before the world. All Priscilla knew was that the last time they had driven very slowly, and that people had stared at them until she felt uncomfortable. Today, however, she was in such high spirits that she didn't even mind going. She was dressed in a new jade-colored redingote with a matching plumed hat. But the fire in her eyes and the blush on her cheeks outshown the handsome new outfit.

The earl must have noticed that, too. For his gaze

48

fanned over her, and something like approval glinted in his eyes.

"Good day, milord." He helped her into his high-perch phaeton, and they set off for the park. She noticed his sideways glances in her direction but was more intent on savoring Geoffrey's compliments. Her painting had always been very important to her, and it was nice to have it recognized.

"London is beginning to agree with you," the earl observed.

"Yes, it is a beautiful city." She was in the mood to be charitable to anything or anyone. Still, she had to admit she was beginning to find London more tolerable. Or maybe it was that she felt comfortable with Mrs. Speers and not so alone anymore. Even the earl seemed less formidable.

As before, the path was choked with carriages. They moved at a snail's pace, but today Priscilla didn't mind. It gave her an opportunity to observe other women—how they dressed, what they said, the way they acted toward men. At first she had looked because she thought those were things she ought to know. Now, however, she was developing curiosity about such things.

"I believe you will be ready to attend some routs shortly," the earl said.

She nodded agreeably. Even that no longer seemed so threatening.

"How go the dance lessons?" the earl asked.

That question dimmed her enthusiasm. Looking at her hands to avoid his gaze, she answered honestly, "I am trying very hard."

He laughed. "You needn't sound so bleak. They don't lop off your head if you are not the best dancer in London."

"That's fortunate."

This time his laughter rumbled up from deep inside him. Priscilla could not determine what was so amusing. Nor was she aware that her quizzical glances up at him from beneath long, curling lashes were full of innocent feminine allure. His laughter died, and something less easily defined appeared in his eyes.

Suddenly self-conscious, she touched the plume of her bonnet. "Is something wrong?"

"No, of course not." Abruptly he turned his attention back to the reins.

What a strange man he was, Priscilla reflected. At times, she almost felt they were friends, or at the very least that he liked her. Then she reminded herself that he was doing all this for the sake of an old debt to her father. At most his feelings for her were that of polite tolerance.

She was absorbed in that unflattering thought until her attention was captured by a blond-haired lady in an elegant barouche.

"She's very pretty," Priscilla said wistfully. Her own dark curls seemed common compared to this woman's blond tresses.

Lord Knole cleared his throat loudly. "Pray do not stare at her. She is not recognized by polite society."

Priscilla turned a curious face up to him. "Why not?"

"It is rumored that she engages in, ahem, unladylike activities."

A number of things flashed through Priscilla's mind. Mrs. Speers had lectured her thoroughly about ladylike behavior. It consisted of not riding one's horse too fast along Rotten Row, keeping one's eyes meekly lowered when being introduced to a peer, and not standing up with a man more than twice for a waltz. "How is she unladylike?"

There was a moment's pause before he said, "She entertains men."

That explanation only served to confuse Priscilla more. Was not the purpose of women in society to entertain with soirees and parties? "I don't understand."

The blond-haired woman fluttered a hand in his direction. "Robert, you wicked man, you have not been to see me in ages. You must call on me immediately. I shall go into a decline if you do not."

Priscilla turned to him. "She seems to know you."

The earl faced stonily ahead. "It would please me if you would stop looking in her direction."

Reluctantly, Priscilla turned away. The woman seemed quite the most interesting person she had come upon in London. Not that she had met many people thus far. Her social life until now had consisted of smiling at those they passed in their jaunts through the park and dining alone with Mrs. Speers and sometimes with Geoffrey.

A coach pulled up alongside their phaeton and a ruddy-faced man smiled up at them. " 'Lo, Robert."

The earl nodded briskly. "James."

The man's gaze went to Priscilla. "I don't believe I have had the pleasure of meeting your lovely companion."

"It's Miss Springton. If you'll pardon me, it's time we returned home." With an expertise that made handling the spirited matched bays look easy, Lord Knole turned the phaeton around and started back toward the house.

Priscilla looked back over her shoulder. "But we just got here," she complained.

"And now we are leaving." He spoke as if he were

talking to a child. "You are not to encourage James Whitley. He is far too fond of imbibing to make any woman a suitable husband."

"I didn't encourage him."

"You smiled at him." He gave her a severe look. "You are to be more discriminating about where you place your smiles. I shall tell you when you may smile. And when you do, pray endeavor to look stern rather than fetching."

With that admonition ringing in her ears, she fell silent. Several minutes later, the earl escorted Priscilla up to Mrs. Speers's door and bundled her inside. She stared resentfully after him as he departed. She had been in a happy frame of mind when he arrived; now she felt quite irritable.

"You've become very mysterious, Robert." Lady Galvestly tapped Lord Knole on the shoulder with her fan. She was a starched older woman who, it was rumored, had once been courted by the Prince Regent.

"How is that?" he asked as he swept her into a graceful curve of the waltz.

"You know very well. You have been seen of late driving in the park with a young lady. No one knows anything whatsoever about her."

"Ah, that."

"Yes, *that*. Give over. Who is she?"

The earl had anticipated such questions. He had no intention of satisfying Lady Galvestly's or anyone else's curiosity on the truth of Priscilla's lineage. "She is connected to my family."

"I know everyone in your family," she pronounced.

He smiled sleekly. "I'm full of surprises."

"Indeed you are." Her fan was brought into play

52

again, this time to tap at his arm. "I do not like young men to be mysterious with me."

The dance ended, and he took his leave with a bow. It proved not to be the last time that evening he was questioned about Priscilla. In fact, he was surprised by the speculation she had generated. Because no one knew who she was, and because she had been seen with him, she had become a woman of mystery and interest.

Over in the corners of the room, the dowagers murmured among themselves that if the gel could attract the attention of the earl, she must be of high social standing. Someone had heard she was from India. The story spread from the little group around the ratafia bowl to the men playing cards in the back salon that she was the daughter of an expatriate English duke and a Hindu princess. The earl, it was said, was smitten.

Happily unaware of this rumor, Lord Knole remained at the dance and stood up with several young ladies. He was not known for spending so much time at parties. But this Season was different. This season he was searching for a wife.

It was time, he had decided, that he have an heir. After all, he was one-and-thirty. If he meant to bring the boy up properly, he could not wait much longer.

Looking around the crowded room, he noted that there were plenty of debutantes to choose from. None seemed to fit his needs. They either simpered, or had nothing to say for themselves, or talked *too* much, or were just plain boring. Eighteen-year-old chits, he was discovering, could be insufferable even when they were diamonds of the first water. He was coming to believe he must broaden his search to include older women—up to the age of four-and-twenty. At that advanced age, of course, he had to be willing to consider a widow.

He finished a contredanse and returned a smiling young lady to her mother. Then he went in search of someone more mature.

He found her almost immediately.

Emily Simpson was standing with several other women. Her burnished red hair framed a lovely oval face. She had been married briefly to a man who had died of brain fever. For the past three years, she had been a quiet, demure widow. This was the first Season she had returned to society.

Walking up to her, he bowed over her hand. "Mrs. Simpson, a pleasure to see you."

She smiled sweetly at him.

Yes, he decided, his choice was made.

Unaware of the tales of intrigue making the rounds about her, Priscilla continued to be instructed by Mrs. Speers and to paint whenever she had the chance.

At the moment, it was midday, and she was seated beside Mrs. Speers on the aging Hepplewhite sofa. They were supposed to be selecting gowns from a stack of fashion plates. But the plates lay neglected on the floor while they sat hip to hip and read *Vathek*.

Priscilla skimmed the page quickly; she was completely absorbed in the fantastic oriental story of black magic.

"We really ought to make some selections for gowns," Mrs. Speers would say from time to time.

"Mmmm," Priscilla would agree, and they would share some more chocolates and read more from the exciting book.

They were thus both occupied when they heard a male voice.

"Good morning, ladies."

Mrs. Speers slapped the book closed and stuck it under a pillow. "Oh, it's only you, Geoffrey."

His smile was full of condescension. "I trust you are in good health?"

"Don't be addlepated, Geoffrey. Of course we are, or we wouldn't be sitting here." Mrs. Speers's words notwithstanding, her voice was full of indulgence. She reached for the fashion plates. "Come tell me if you don't think this walking dress in a water green crepe would look perfect on Priscilla."

He approached but scarcely glanced at the plate. His gaze was on Priscilla. "Anything would look remarkable on Miss Springton."

Priscilla flushed. She was unused to compliments, but finding that she liked them very well indeed. Even Lord Knole had commented on her gown yesterday, a fact which had pleased her.

"Yes, she has a lovely figure," Mrs. Speers agreed absently. Sighing, she popped a chocolate into her mouth. "If only she could master the boulanger."

"She will in time. Besides, what matters it how she dances when she is such a superb artist?" He smiled in her direction. "By the by, Miss Springton, a friend saw my painting and liked it so well that he inquired whether you might do one for him."

"She shan't have time for painting once she begins attending routs," Mrs. Speers said crisply.

"Of course she will, my dear aunt. One always has time for the things that please one most. Besides, she is not attending parties yet."

"I should like to paint something for your friend," Priscilla said shyly.

"Naturally he would pay you well."

"Oh, that isn't necessary," she objected quickly. "I paint because I enjoy it. I would do it as a favor."

"Then he will buy you canvases. I think he had a particular painting in mind. I will bring you something to copy from."

"Very well, Geoffrey," Mrs. Speers said, "but now you must go along. Priscilla and I have to finish selecting her wardrobe."

Geoffrey cast a sardonic glance at the book sticking out from beneath the pillow, executed a short bow, and departed.

Anxious to begin work on a new painting, and eager to see what Geoffrey would bring her to copy, Priscilla awaited his return. When she heard the front door open the next day, she ran downstairs to greet him.

Midway down, she halted. It was only the earl. He glanced up, startled by her sudden entry.

"Oh, it's you," she said.

The smile that had begun on his lips died, and the curve of his shoulders stiffened. "You were expecting someone else?"

Priscilla put aside her disappointment. "Yes, but it doesn't signify. Were we to go for a drive today? I had forgotten."

Lord Knole looked tall and straight in a blue superfine coat. But his face was a cold mask. "We had not made plans, but I thought you might like to since it's such a pleasant day."

"That would be fine," she said without noticeable enthusiasm. She was afraid she would miss Geoffrey if she left, but the earl's forbidding look prevented her from declining his offer. She glanced down at her lavender gown and decided it would be appropriate. "I shall get my pelisse and bonnet."

Five minutes later, she was back downstairs

wearing a dark purple pelisse and a matching bonnet with a low, velvet brim. She was getting used to the somber and washed out colors the English seemed so fond of, but still missed the bright, pretty shades she had worn in India.

The earl offered a stiff elbow, and she accepted it. Together they walked down the short flight of steps to his phaeton. He handed her up into it and started off. They rode in silence for several minutes.

Finally, he said, "It is time you attend a rout. There is one on Friday that will suit our purposes very well."

Apprehension made Priscilla's skin prickly. Memories of her one foray into polite society still made her uneasy. She dreaded facing a crowd of strange and unfriendly people. "Is it to be a large party?" she asked tentatively.

"No, it will be quite small, but there will be dancing." He skillfully guided the horses around a slow-moving carriage before continuing, "How does your dancing progress?"

She sighed. "Poorly."

"We must see what we can do about that."

They entered the park, and a man on a prancing black stallion rode up beside them.

"Knole, splendid to see you." The equestrian's eyes fastened on her and lingered there.

In fact, Priscilla thought everyone in the park was looking at her. Surely it was only her imagination. Why should they concern themselves with her when there were so many others present, including the pretty blond woman in the blue barouche?

"Sir Ames, this is Miss Springton," the earl said.

The newcomer raised his high-crowned hat politely. "Of the Stafford Springtons?"

"No, they are the Springhams," the earl said. "You will excuse me, Sir Ames, but my horses are growing restless. Good day." He left the horseman behind with a deft movement of the reins that took them around a large tree.

"I don't believe Sir Ames was through talking to us."

Lord Knole laughed briefly. "Or looking."

Not knowing what to say about that, she remained silent. She had noted the masculine approval in Sir Ames's glance. In truth, it made her feel rosy with pleasure.

As their drive continued, others glanced in their direction.

"People seem to be watching us," she murmured.

"Yes," the earl agreed calmly. "They are curious about you. Don't worry," the earl drawled sardonically. "You will be a nine days' wonder. Next week they will have something or someone else to occupy their thoughts."

"Oh," she said in a small voice, her spirits dampened.

"Now," he continued briskly, "it is time that we returned to Mrs. Speers. I should like to see you dance."

Priscilla tensed. He wanted to watch her dance? The thought of the earl standing to the side and observing critically made her nervous. Sitting silently, she tried desperately to remember the steps to every dance she had learned thus far.

When they arrived at Mrs. Speers's house, that good woman was thrilled at the prospect of showing off Priscilla's progress. The older woman sat down at the pianoforte and experimentally thumped a few keys. "Why don't we start with the waltz?" she suggested. "*One*, two, three," she counted loudly, hitting the first note hard. "Priscilla, pet, you're not dancing."

It was true. Priscilla stood helplessly in the middle of the floor. How could she dance around the room by herself with Lord Knole looking on? She did that when it was only she and Lady Speers, but this was another matter altogether.

The earl must have taken pity. "A partner would make things easier," he said and walked over to her. Expertly, he cupped his right arm around her waist and extended his left into a straight line out at the side. "Now, then, is this better?"

She nodded woodenly. In reality, his nearness only made it harder for her to concentrate. The smell of soap and leather interfered with her thinking, and the touch of his large, warm hands on her body made her self-conscious and uncertain. It also made her feel small and slightly breathless.

Mrs. Speers pounded on the keys. "Now, then, *one*, two, three."

The counting was unnecessary, for the earl expertly guided her into the steps of the dance.

"You're too stiff, Miss Springton. Relax."

Priscilla tried but couldn't.

"Think of something funny," the earl suggested. "Or ridiculous."

She stared up at him, but nothing funny came to mind. In fact, all she could think about was the handsome set of his features and how his eyes looked even greener up close. She had never been this near him before. If they moved only a few inches, their lips would touch. At that outrageous thought, she stumbled.

He caught her easily.

"You're certain they won't play the minuet?" she asked forlornly.

His soft laughter soothed her. "Quite certain. Let us try the waltz again, shall we?"

In the end, it was his patience that helped Priscilla's dancing improve. He was willing to execute the steps over and over. Gradually she began to relax. When she finally performed a turn without a misstep, she smiled triumphantly up at him.

"Well done," he murmured.

Priscilla didn't mean to flirt, but when their eyes met, a sparkle crept into hers. It was the excitement of the moment, she told herself. She could feel the pink flush on her cheeks; she was actually *enjoying* dancing with Lord Knole. Judging from his bemused smile, he was enjoying himself as well.

Perhaps not, though, for abruptly his expression turned cold, and he said, "I think that's enough."

She tried to hide her disappointment.

Mrs. Speers stopped playing and came over to join them, effusive in her praise and gratitude. "Thank you ever so much, milord. You are the best dancing instructor she could possibly have had."

"She shall have plenty of chances to practice at the Wilkinson's rout," he said briskly.

"Yes, milord."

"She needs further tutoring, of course, but I think she can pass in polite company. Pray have her ready to go by nine."

Priscilla felt suddenly foolish. The way the earl spoke of her, she might not even have been present. It occurred to her that the dancing and new clothes were all to the end of finding her a man—someone other than the earl—to wed. To feel a warm glow in his presence was humiliating, considering that he wished nothing more than to see her married to another. Once she was wed, he would have no further contact with her.

Mrs. Speers continued to gush. "I am persuaded it will be a very grand and exciting evening. Priscilla should have several new gowns ready by then."

"Have her wear something suitably modest. And white. She may be old, but she is still a debutante."

Color stung into Priscilla's cheeks. Old, he had said.

Turning to her, he executed a polite bow and took his leave.

Priscilla watched him go in stony silence.

Chapter 5

"We shall stay only a brief time," Lord Knole informed her as the carriage jolted to a halt in front of a Palladian-style mansion.

Priscilla, resigned to her fate, nodded.

"And remember what I told you about India."

Her lips tightened. "I remember." She was to speak as little of it as possible. In point of fact, she could not conceive what she *was* to talk about should anyone engage her in conversation. Her family was not to be discussed. Her relationship with the earl was to be left vague. If India was mentioned, she was to change the subject. Why? Any man who courted her would surely learn the details of her past anyway. Besides, she was proud of her parents and of having lived in India.

Lord Knole helped her alight from the carriage. Mrs. Speers was right behind them. Priscilla held her long sarcenet gown off the ground and kept her head down, looking at the toes of her satin slippers as she mounted the marble steps. It would all be over shortly, and she could go back to Mrs. Speers's house and perhaps paint awhile before going to bed, she promised herself.

They were met at the door by a young footman who took their wraps. He looked flustered.

"What are all the coaches out front?" Mrs. Speers asked an elderly woman they met at the door. "I understood it was a small rout."

"*Everyone* is here. They say someone important is coming."

"I wonder who?"

Priscilla didn't think Mrs. Speers was talking to her, so she didn't answer. Besides, she hadn't the faintest idea of anyone who would be here, never mind someone important. But it did add a touch of interest to the evening and gave her something to think about besides her nervousness.

Moments later, Priscilla, the earl, and Mrs. Speers stood at the edge of a great hall. Its arched ceiling was alive with paintings of saints and cherubs. Priscilla would like to have stood there and studied the artwork, but already the earl was drawing her forward.

"Ghastly, isn't it?" he muttered beside her. "Lord Wilkinson's father went through a religious period. He had the good sense to quit this earth before he ruined the whole of the house." In a louder voice, he said, "Lady Wilkinson, how charming to see you. You remember Mrs. Speers, and this is my guest, Miss Springton."

The stout woman nodded pleasantly toward Mrs. Speers, but her attention was on Priscilla. "Miss Springton," she repeated, as if she wished to brand the name in her mind. "I am honored that you have come to our humble rout."

Priscilla looked around. Humble? The room was aglitter with gems and finery. "It looks very grand to me," she answered truthfully.

"You're too kind. But I'm sure it's not on the

scale of entertaining done in India. You *are* from India, are you not?''

Priscilla threw a questioning glance at the earl, who nodded almost imperceptibly. ''Yes, I have lived there.''

''Ah.'' that seemed to affirm something in her ladyship's mind. ''I have heard tales the Maharaja Ranjit Singh scatters gold upon his guests, and that his cups and decanters and bed are of solid gold.''

Priscilla had heard as much herself, although, of course, she had never met him. ''His body servants protect their beards with tissues of gold filaments,'' she added, having heard that somewhere as well.

''How fascinating. You must have seen a great deal. You and I shall have a nice coze sometime, and you can tell me *all* about yourself.''

The earl smoothly interrupted. ''I did not expect so many people tonight.''

''It was to have been a small affair. Then news that you and Miss Springton were coming got about and suddenly dozens of people requested invitations.'' She lifted her hands in a delicate display of helplessness. ''What could I do but invite them?''

Lady Wilkinson put an arm around Priscilla and ushered her further into the room. ''There are so many people I wish you to meet that I cannot think where to start.''

Priscilla looked back for Mrs. Speers, but she had found someone she knew and was caught up in her own conversation. She paid no attention as Priscilla left.

Proudly, like a brood hen showing off a chick, Lady Wilkinson led her to a group of dignified-looking older women. ''Ladies,'' she announced importantly, ''this is Miss Springton.''

A hush fell as every pair of eyes in the circle turned in her direction. Priscilla stood self-consciously while she was inspected from head to foot. Then gracious smiles and murmurs of welcome filled the silence.

"How charming to meet you at last, Miss Springton."

"I have seen you in the carriage with Lord Knole. I'm so pleased you came tonight, Miss Springton."

"Do sit down and join us, Miss Springton."

There was a significant amount of shuffling as the ladies made a place for her. Priscilla had the impression it was important to more than one that she sit beside that particular lady. In fact, something very like a quarrel occurred between two genteel ladies trying to decide whom Priscilla should sit next to.

"She can sit here, Martha."

"Of course, but the air is so much fresher over here, Estelle."

"I don't mind where I sit," Priscilla said. Privately, she reflected again how very strange the British were. At the last soiree no one had paid the least attention to her. Suddenly people seemed eager to be with her. She could not think what had changed in the interim.

She was pulled down into a chair beside the woman called Martha. "Now, dear, tell me about your family. I don't believe I am familiar with the Springtons."

"There's very little to tell, really. Papa and Mama have lived abroad for a number of years."

"Yes, yes, dear, but tell me about your relatives—your connections."

Priscilla hesitated. "Well, I—"

"Martha, pray don't press the child so. I'm sure

her family is impeccable. She is, after all, here with the earl."

"Yes," Lady Wilkinson agreed and added a significantly withering look at Martha.

"I should much rather hear about all of you," Priscilla said.

It was, apparently, the first time the dowagers and matrons had been asked about themselves in some time. After an initial hesitation, each proved more than happy to talk. In the resulting explosion of chatter, Priscilla learned that one had twelve grandchildren, that another wrote verse, and that a third woman was doing a needlepoint sampler based on a medieval tapestry. Lady Wilkinson confided that she could play anything on the pianoforte after she had heard it once.

"How splendid," Priscilla murmured to the group just as Lord Knole appeared. "The ladies have been telling me about themselves," she informed him.

He bowed courteously. "I'm sure that was most interesting."

"Indeed it was," Priscilla agreed. She liked her new acquaintances.

The earl smiled, making each woman in the circle feel she was the sole recipient of his smile. "I wonder if I might borrow Miss Springton for the boulanger?"

Lady Wilkinson beamed at him. "Yes, of course. She's such a sweet child."

Others added their agreement as she left with Lord Knole.

"You appear to have captivated them," the earl said dryly. "I thought you might be in need of rescue. Where is that addlepated Mrs. Speers? She should be with you instead of throwing you to those wolves."

"They were very kind," Priscilla objected.

"Humph."

As they reached the edge of the floor, Priscilla's nerve deserted her. "Must we stand up for the boulanger? Perhaps we could wait for a country dance or a—"

"Don't worry. You did fine yesterday."

"But there weren't dozens of people watching me then." She edged closer to him, suddenly aware that everyone *was* watching her. The enormity of the situation dawned on her that *she* was the person that people had come to see.

"Don't concern yourself with them. Concentrate on the dance."

They remained on the dance floor while the opening chords of the music sounded. Her gaze went once again to the tips of her satin slippers.

"Look at me," he commanded softly.

She obeyed. As the dance began, she moved woodenly with the music. Her gaze remained fixed on his. Surprisingly, she saw something reassuring in the clear green depths of his eyes. Slowly the noise and the crowd receded from her thoughts until she and the earl were dancing alone. The longer the music continued, the less it felt like dancing. Priscilla didn't have to think. Her body simply responded. It was like floating.

Then the dance ended.

"I think we did passably well," he said.

"Yes," she said breathlessly.

They had moved apart, but their gazes stayed fixed on each other. It was as if they both had something they wanted to say but neither could find the words.

Then someone was at her elbow. "I say, Robert,

why don't you introduce me to your lovely companion?"

The intrusion broke the spell of the moment.

The earl turned a cordial smile on the handsome man with the mustache. "Lord Wexford, this is Miss Springton."

The other man bowed over her hand. "I'm charmed. I should like nothing better than to stand up with you for the next set. Are you free?"

She nodded, feeling more confident in her ability.

The earl melted away into the crowd; her partner continued smiling urbanely at her. "I daresay you are aware of the stir you have created," he said as they began a set of country dances. "People shamelessly wrangled invitations for tonight once rumor circulated that you were to be present."

"Why?" she asked simply. The English were such a peculiar race. Why should it matter that she was here this evening?

"Because you are pretty and because the *ton* knows so little about you."

It still made little sense to her.

He looked toward the edge of the dance floor. "I see it was quite a stroke of luck that I was able to stand up with you at all. From the looks of the men gathering around Robert, you won't lack for dancing partners this evening."

Priscilla glanced toward the earl. He was indeed surrounded by men. She didn't know whether to be flattered or terrified.

Mrs. Speers stood on the other side of the wide dance floor. When the dance ended, Lord Wexford escorted her back to her chaperone.

It wasn't long before men began approaching, dredging up ancient acquaintances with Mrs. Speers or boldly admitting to not knowing Priscilla's chaperone, but insisting they were great, good friends of the earl. Soon every dance was spoken for.

For the next dance, Priscilla was escorted onto the floor by a tall man in a uniform. He informed her that he had lived in India. "I don't recollect meeting you there," he said.

"We were in a remote area." Glancing at the earl, she recalled his admonition against divulging too much about herself. "I really don't know if I should talk about it," she said hastily.

He pondered that heavily. "I see. I understand about these sensitive matters since I am in the military myself. I certainly wouldn't ask you to betray country and king."

She cast him a confused but grateful smile.

By the end of the evening, Priscilla had met scores of people and had danced until her feet ached. All in all, it was a wonderful evening. Once she overcame her apprehension about the attention focused on her, she had found that she enjoyed having men murmur compliments and dance attendance on her. She couldn't remember when she had felt so important or happy.

Mrs. Speers shared in her triumph.

Only the earl was quiet on the drive home.

"Was it not a successful evening?" Priscilla prodded, anxious to hear him compliment her and share in the glow of her success.

"Perhaps," he said cryptically. "I'd as lief you had not spread the word your father was engaged in secret work for the king, but I daresay what's done is done."

Priscilla was too pleased to have her enthusiasm dampened. Whimsically curling and uncurling a ringlet around her finger, she sank back against

69

the squabs, smiling at the memory of flattering things that men had said to her. England might not be so bad after all.

Emily Simpson was dressed in a demure green muslin gown when Lord Knole called on her the day following the soiree. She received him in the drawing room of her family's Tudor home. Her mother was present, sitting discreetly in the corner of the dark, paneled room and working, or pretending to work, on her tatting.

Emily escorted the earl to a ramrod straight chair that proved to be as uncomfortable as he had feared.

She folded her hands primly in her lap and waited for him to speak.

"It was a large affair last evening, did you not think?" he asked politely.

"Quite large, milord."

She was shy, he told himself, which accounted for why she did not volunteer more conversation. Reserve was a becoming quality in a woman and something he should like in his wife.

"Will you be going to Almack's this evening?" he inquired.

"I believe so."

"And you, Lord Knole," her mother interrupted, looking up from her handiwork to smile at him. "You have not attended Almack's yet this Season. Will you go this evening?"

"Yes." He shifted in the awkward chair but was unable to find a more comfortable position.

"I daresay you must be present if your ward means to go."

He cleared his throat carefully. If Mrs. Simpson assumed Priscilla was his ward, that was as good a term as any. It was the other part of her statement that worried him. "Miss Springton has no plans to go to Almack's." And would be turned away at the door if she attempted to enter, he added silently. She would never pass the exacting scrutiny of the patronesses. Once the facts of her family's background became known, he questioned whether he could even continue to take her as his guest to other social events.

"Indeed?" Lady Simpson inclined her white head quizzically. "She seemed to enjoy some success last night. I expected her to attend this evening."

To say she enjoyed some success was to understate the case. He should have felt enormously pleased at her acceptance, instead of feeling this vague, unexplainable sense of unease. But, as he had told Priscilla in the carriage on the way home, it would all pass quickly enough, particularly once people's curiosity had been satisfied and the real facts about her began to emerge. "I don't believe she will attend," he restated, and turned his attention back to Emily. "That shade of green looks particularly charming on you."

"Thank you, sir."

He struggled along with further conversation for a few more minutes, then rose to take his leave. Bowing over her hand, he said, "With your permission, I should like to call on you tomorrow and take you for a drive through the park."

"I should like that." She looked at him for the first time and added hesitantly, "I hope it shan't be too vigorous a drive."

"Nothing of the sort. The pace shall be just as you say and not a step faster." Her delicacy made him feel strong and protective. He wouldn't dream of oversetting her by letting the horses have their heads.

71

On the way out the door, it occurred to him that speed did not daunt Priscilla. In fact, the few times the horses had reached a brisk trot, he had noted a gleam of excitement in her eyes. Really, she had looked quite fetching. Resolutely he reminded himself that Priscilla's enthusiasm was unacceptable.

Emily was gently reared and not at all accustomed to such things, which was quite as it should be. Her gentleness spoke all the better for the sort of mother she would make. She would take care to see that any female children she bore did not become hoydens. How Priscilla Springton's daughters would turn out was anyone's guess.

"I have the ace, Mrs. Speers," Priscilla said, "so you don't win after all."

"Pooh!" The older woman tossed down her cards in disgust.

"Our little houseguest is quite adept at this game," Geoffrey noted with a smile at her. He seemed to enjoy the game even though he was losing.

More than once Priscilla had caught his gaze lingering on her. It might be unmaidenly, but she was flattered by his attention.

The threesome were seated in the breakfast room just off the tiny garden where the caretaker was even now clipping the hedgerow. The French doors were open to allow a breeze and, alas, the occasional flying insect, into the room.

Priscilla was shuffling the cards when the earl appeared. He was dressed in the fawn coat, white unmentionables, and pure black Hessians he had worn once on their drive to the park. It was an outfit she found particularly handsome.

"Good day, milord," Mrs. Speers greeted him cheerfully.

Lord Knole nodded to all, but his gaze rested on Geoffrey. "I don't believe I've had the honor."

"Oh, this is my nephew, Geoffrey Speers," Mrs. Speers said. Brief pleasantries were exchanged before the earl's gaze returned to Priscilla.

He looked at the cards in her hand and lifted one eyebrow. "Gaming?"

She smiled brightly.

Geoffrey looked sheepish. "I assure you it is the tamest of games. We were just ready to stop," he added hastily.

"Not while I'm winning," Priscilla objected.

"You really should not indulge in such pastimes," the earl said.

Priscilla sensed he meant to be sharp, but the light of amusement was beginning to flicker in his eyes.

"I shall tell my partners you think as much when I begin to lose," she said pertly.

A laugh escaped him. "You are incorrigible."

Judging from the humor in his voice, he didn't mean it in a bad way. Amusement changed his voice somehow—made it gravelly, but in an appealing way.

"Would you care to join us?" she suggested.

He hesitated. "Since you are, after a fashion, my ward, I'm not sure it would be seemly for me to join you in a game of chance."

"Or wise for you, my dear Miss Springton," Geoffrey drawled. "The earl is known to be bang up to the mark when it comes to gambling."

Priscilla frowned at Geoffrey. "Bang up to the mark? What does that mean?"

73

"You must be bamming me. Everyone knows what that means. You've never heard the phrase?"

"The child has been living in India," Mrs. Speers reminded her nephew. Turning to Priscilla, she explained, "It means superior."

"Then why didn't he simply say so?" Priscilla asked tartly. "Whatever is the point of saying one thing when one means another?" The earl's slow-dawning, indulgent smile only made her more indignant.

"We've had several callers since the soiree, milord," Mrs. Speers said in an obvious effort to change the subject.

"Indeed?" He pulled out a chair and sat down across from Priscilla.

"Oh my, yes. Sir Humphrey came and brought quite a lovely nosegay. And Mr. Casey was here. And Austin Gregory."

"Discourage Casey," the earl said flatly. "He's too old. And Sir Humphrey is too given to following the horses. In truth, I can't like you encouraging Austin Gregory, either."

Priscilla had come to exactly the same conclusions about the three men who had called on her. Yet even though she had no interest in them, she disliked having her only suitors found so wanting. "I find Mr. Casey charming," she said obstinately.

"Entirely too old for you. He's practically in his dotage."

Priscilla might have argued the point further but didn't know what dotage meant. She had to content herself with demanding briskly, "Are we playing cards or not?"

They did. Halfway through the hand, she regretted the suggestion. She disliked losing, and she most particularly disliked losing to the earl. She glared up at him when he won yet another hand. He grinned unapologetically at her. Tilting her nose upward, she returned her attention to her cards.

"Thank heavens you didn't suggest playing for money," Geoffrey said when Lord Knole won yet another round.

The earl turned to the other man. "I confess that you have me at a disadvantage. You seem to know about me. I know your name but little else about you."

"I have a small estate in Wiltshire. I'm a bit of a ramshackle landlord, I must own," Geoffrey confided with a disarming smile. "I spend a deal of my time in London."

The earl nodded. "Of late I haven't devoted the time I should to my own estates."

Would he be doing that now if it were not for her? Priscilla wondered. Was his very presence in London an onerous task undertaken strictly because of her? Stains of pink crept into her cheeks at that thought. She didn't like the thought of being a burden and an inconvenience.

"You won that hand, Priscilla."

She turned her attention back to the game. But every now and then, her gaze went to Lord Knole, and she wondered exactly how unpleasant it was for him to be responsible for her. Well, she would solve that quickly enough. She would marry soon, and he would be shed of her.

"By the by, Miss Springton," Lord Knole said, "do you have any drawing room accomplishments? Perhaps you sing or play the pianoforte?" He seemed to speak without much hope.

"I paint."

He dismissed that with a disinterested nod and addressed himself to Mrs. Speers. "I know she's well

75

past the age when a young lady should learn such things, but perhaps you could engage a teacher for piano lessons or voice lessons. Even if she plays only a little or sings only passably well, it will give her a look of some polish. She will undoubtedly be asked at some gathering or another to perform."

"I'm sure I can find someone to instruct her," Mrs. Speers said brightly.

"Splendid. I shall leave it in your capable hands." He won the game. Rising, he pushed back his chair. "I shall take my leave."

"A pleasure to have seen you, milord," the older woman said.

"Yes," Priscilla managed to agree, but she chafed over the fact that he had taken no interest whatsoever in her painting. The earl might not appreciate her talent, but that didn't prevent her from going up to her room and taking great care to put the finishing touches on a painting for Geoffrey. *He* appreciated her art even if the earl did not.

Chapter 6

"The wig, Miss Priscilla, will you need it this evening?"

"No, Maria."

The English maid Esther had come down with a nasty cough, and Priscilla's Indian maid was once again in attendance on her as she prepared for a small dinner party.

"In fact," Priscilla said, "we shan't need the wig ever again. People here do not wear them."

"No, they do not appear to," Maria agreed.

As the small, dark-skinned woman hunted for gloves and a fan, Priscilla sat on the edge of the bed. Mama had been wrong about fashion being constant. It changed from year to year. Even, Priscilla suspected, from month to month. Dances changed, too. The minuet had gone out of style.

The unhappy thought occurred to Priscilla that Mama had been wrong because she had never been part of the elite set of people who came to London to be presented. All Mama knew about the *ton* was what she read and what she imagined. The reality was far more complex, Priscilla was discovering. She was also learning that titles dictated who mattered more than how much money one possessed. Did that mean that her father was not important? Because his name had carried so much weight in India, she had assumed the same would be true in England. But she was coming to the uncomfortable realization that the earl was a far more important person that her father.

"Here are the gloves." Her maid laid out a pair of tan kid gloves.

"I wanted the white ones, Maria. The ones with mother-of-pearl buttons."

"Yes, you did say that, didn't you?"

As the slim young woman turned back to the task of finding the proper gloves, Priscilla watched her with sharpened curiosity. Her maid seemed preoccupied. Now that Priscilla thought about it, Maria had seemed distracted the other day as well. "Is something wrong, Maria?"

"Oh no, ma'am," the maid said quickly.

But Priscilla wasn't convinced. Gently she probed, "Do you miss India?"

"Sometimes, but it is very pleasant in London, too," Maria said in her precise, accented English.

"I am beginning to feel the same way," Priscilla confided. "At times I miss India, but sometimes it is not so bad to be here."

Their conversation was interrupted when Mrs. Speers fluttered into the room. "You must hurry, dear. The carriage is waiting."

Priscilla's gaze went to the small ormolu clock on the mantle. "But it's only eight. You said we wouldn't leave until nine."

"Did I? Dear me, well, I meant eight, and we must go immediately." Skirts swishing, she turned and left.

Priscilla sighed. It was not the first time Mrs. Speers's memory had failed her. In truth, her chaperone was a bit flighty, but Priscilla was careful not to mention this to Lord Knole. After all, he had selected Mrs. Speers. She wouldn't want him to think she was criticizing his choice. Besides, she dealt well with Mrs. Speers.

Maria helped her into a high-waisted gown of parchment-colored silk striped in maroon. The short sleeves were caught up in a drapery to the shoulders. Priscilla fussed with the sleeves while the maid hunted out a necklace of gold and garnets.

She was fastening on the necklace when a servant appeared to say the horses must not be kept standing overlong. Mrs. Speers returned to hurry her along. "It won't do to come in late while someone is performing at the pianoforte."

"Yes, yes," Priscilla said and rushed from the room. As a consequence of her haste, she didn't have time to arrange her hair properly. Curling dark wisps framed her face in a way that made her look girlish. Her eyes were bright and her cheeks flushed from rushing around.

Twenty minutes later she alighted in front of Lindham House. Tonight, at least, she did not feel nervous. As she handed her pelisse to a servant, she heard a woman nearby observe, "She's a beauty," and her spirits were further uplifted.

"Not in the ordinary way of things, but charming in her own way," a male replied.

Mrs. Speers leaned close and whispered excitedly, "They're talking about you."

Priscilla's color went even higher, which served to make her eyes brighter. With Mrs. Speers beside her, she proceeded into the salon where rows of chairs were set up. A few people stood around the back of the room chatting. It was not a large affair, but those present seemed to be watching her. She might have slipped into a chair and sat with her eyes demurely cast down had she not seen the earl.

His gaze on her made her bolder. Lifting her head, she smiled regally at the assemblage, treating them as if they had come solely to see her. As well they might have, she reflected without humility. Stopping at the nearest person whom she recognized—a portly young man—she extended a hand.

"Sir Groshans, how nice to see you." She smiled prettily.

"And you, Miss Springton."

The earl was still watching, she noted out of the corner of her eye. Broadening her smile, Priscilla searched for something more to say.

Fortunately, Sir Groshans spoke. He was obviously pleased by her attention. "Everyone was wondering whether you'd come. Hoping you would, I should say."

"How kind of them."

"You being the daughter of a maharaja and all, they're naturally curious. I even left the play at White's early m'self to come," he confided. "Course, I was losing anyway," he noted regretfully.

Mrs. Speers tugged at Priscilla's arm. "Do come along, pet, Melanie Rainey is going to entertain in a moment, and we must find chairs."

Mrs. Speers marched up to the front row, and Priscilla followed. The music began. Sitting with her hands folded in her lap, Priscilla listened to a pretty girl sing a lament of forsaken love. The song went on much too long. Melanie, for all her fresh-faced charm, had a poor singing voice.

There was an appropriate amount of polite applause when she was done. She was followed by a procession of young ladies who entertained with a variety of songs and musical selections. Unfortunately, none of them was very gifted. The room was hot and the selections boring. As time passed, Priscilla had a hard time keeping her eyes open. Glancing at the glazed expressions around her, she saw others were having similar difficulties.

An interlude at the harp ground to a close, and Mrs. Lindham stepped forward. "I have not yet asked her, but I'm sure Miss Springton could be prevailed upon to entertain us."

Priscilla sat rigidly upright.

Mrs. Speers nudged her. "Go up to the front and do something."

"What shall I do?" she whispered back.

"Anything!"

The whole room was watching her. She must do something. Slowly, she got to her feet and moistened her dry lips with the tip of her tongue. Stiffly she approached the pianoforte and turned to face the crowd. Funny how there seemed to be more people now that she was standing in the front of the room. She glanced around at Melanie and the recent harpist and a dozen others. They had all taken their turns. As bad as she might have found their performances, they had been able to do *something*. What was *she* going to do?

It dashed through Priscilla's mind to sit down at the pianoforte and simply move her fingers across the keys. Some music was bound to result. Perhaps people might even be fooled into thinking she could play. Then her eyes fell on Lord Knole, and she knew she couldn't hope to carry that off.

What could she do?

"Do you need anything?" Mrs. Lindham asked helpfully. "We have more musical instruments. What do you play?"

People stirred in the crowd and leaned forward

for a better view. They were clearly intent on hearing her reply.

She had to say something. There was only one thing she did know how to do in the way of performing. "I do magic," she said softly and lifted her head, defying anyone to laugh.

It must have worked, because a hush fell over the crowd.

"Magic," Mrs. Lindham repeated.

"I need cards." Priscilla refused to ponder whether the guests would consider magic a womanly accomplishment. Instead, she concentrated on trying to remember the one trick she had learned well as a child. Her father had shown it to her when she was fourteen years old. She had only attempted it a few times since then.

Cards were produced. She held them up for the audience to see, just the way Papa had done when she was a child. Then she shuffled them, fanned the top cards, and asked an aged duke in the front row to select a card by how far down it was from the top. She held a card behind the fan in a position that couldn't be seen. Then she squared the deck and asked him to tell how far down the card was.

"Four," he said in a querulous voice.

She dealt four cards from the top, laying aside the fourth. "That should be your card. Turn it over."

He did.

"Is that the card you selected?" she asked.

"No. Mine was the five of hearts."

"Oh, it couldn't have been. I put the five of hearts in my pocket five minutes ago." She put her hand into her pocket and brought out the hidden fifth card.

Then she waited.

82

After a second of silence, a few murmurs were heard. Then applause. It was not resounding, but there was some. "Do something else," Mrs. Lindham suggested.

Priscilla struggled to recall another trick and was able to perform it, this time making a card disappear and reappear in Lord Wensell's pocket. He was astonished, and the audience amused. After one final trick, Priscilla escaped back to her seat. The audience was warm in their applause, and she was feeling rather proud of herself.

She was not to feel that way for long. One quick glance toward the earl showed that he was sitting rigidly upright, his face a study in taut, disapproving lines.

"Lord Knole is unhappy," Priscilla whispered to her chaperone.

Mrs. Speers looked toward him, then patted Priscilla reassuringly. "Never mind, we shall leave as soon as the evening is over, and he won't have a chance to speak to you."

Alas, it was not to be. When Priscilla and her chaperone entered the carriage, he climbed in beside them. The sidelights of the carriage revealed his angry jawline. He glared at Priscilla. "What was the meaning of that singularly ridiculous display you gave tonight?"

"They asked me to do something," she said defensively.

"They didn't request that you perform magic like some gypsy. I would ask you to remember that your reason for being in London is to find a suitable mate. What sort of impression do you think you left on the men who were present tonight?"

"Some of them seemed diverted," Mrs. Speers put in.

"We don't wish to divert people," the earl said tightly. "We want to impress them with the fact Miss Springton would make a suitable wife." He pushed the door open and climbed out. "Pray see to having the chit learn some *proper* accomplishments, Mrs. Speers."

That said, he stalked away.

"He's a wretched person. I am ever so glad I didn't have to marry him," Priscilla said angrily. But her stomach felt knotted, and even she recognized it was hurt pride speaking.

Mrs. Speers signaled to the driver to return them to the house. "Tomorrow," she noted as they alighted in front of her modest house, "we shall find someone to give you voice lessons. How hard can it be to learn a song or two?" she asked cheerily.

Perhaps he had been too hard on Priscilla, Lord Knole reflected the next day as he set off at a smart pace for Mrs. Speers's house. He would take Priscilla for a drive in the park to make amends. While it might not have been wise for her to perform magic, he doubted she had committed an irredeemable sin. People would forget about it in time, and it might not hurt her acceptability.

Feeling magnanimous, he mounted the steps of Mrs. Speers's house and rapped briskly on the door with the head of his cane. A harried maid answered on the second knock.

"Is Miss Springton at home?"

"In the parlor, milord." She took his hat and rushed off.

The earl heard voices before he reached the little blue-and-white parlor. A profusion of flowers sat about on the mantle, on the shelves and on the floor.

Calling cards littered the silver tray on a table inside the door.

"Good afternoon, milord," Mrs. Speers said brightly. "Come sit on the sofa. We've only just gotten a rest from company. Men have been calling all morning."

One dark eyebrow lifted. "Indeed."

"They brought me flowers," Priscilla informed him proudly.

"Indeed," he repeated dryly.

"Lord Newsome himself called," Mrs. Speers said. "And him a duke, no less."

"And the Marquis of Greenfield was here," Priscilla noted happily.

The earl was silent. He should be enormously pleased that Priscilla boasted peers of the realm among her callers. Instead, he felt . . . what? Threatened? Unhappy? Of course not. He felt cautious. Those men must have come out of curiosity rather than a serious wish to court.

"Did you know that the marquis can also perform magic?" Priscilla asked. "He's very good. He showed me several new tricks, and he brought me those lovely yellow primroses."

"Sir Spencer brought the tearoses," Mrs. Speers noted. "I think our Priscilla is doing very well. She has attracted some eminently eligible men."

"I'm pleased," the earl said tautly. But the duke was not the right man for Priscilla. He was colorless and would never be able to control a high-spirited chit like Priscilla. The Marquis of Greenfield was an entirely different story. He was a likable man who was well thought of by his fellows. He maintained excellent stables, played a decent hand of whist, and was discreet in his affairs with women. He would be a superior husband for any

85

woman. Of course, he would never seriously consider Priscilla, the earl was certain, and he might as well disabuse her of that notion right now.

"Not every gentleman who pays a call means to offer marriage," he said. "It's highly unlikely someone like the marquis would. Frankly, he would require a wife of gentler birth."

Mrs. Speers looked offended. "He was most attentive."

Priscilla nodded smug agreement.

Drat the chit, she could at least have the grace to be humble at being honored by the attention of such well-placed men. Considering her true circumstances, she was fortunate indeed to have attracted such highly placed callers.

He turned abruptly to the older woman. "Have you found a piano or voice teacher yet?"

"Yes, milord. She will have her first lesson tomorrow."

"Good." It would give Priscilla something to occupy her mind besides gloating over the number of suitors she had attracted. Although why that should annoy him so, he was at a loss to explain.

The earl left Mrs. Speers's and went directly to Emily Simpson's house. No flowers crowded her parlor, he noted as he was shown into that room. He sat beside Emily on the sofa. Her mother sat directly across from them. Emily was attentive to his remarks and murmured appropriate responses, but initiated little conversation on her own. That was as it should be, Lord Knole reflected, instead of the way it had been at Mrs. Speers's. Priscilla had actually boasted. A lady was, above all things, humble.

"Perhaps we might ride in Hyde Park tomorrow," he suggested to Emily.

"I should like that if the wind is not too high."

He looked at her blankly. This was London, not the North Sea. The winds rarely reached more than breeze stage. A moment of doubt assailed him. Was it foolhardy to consider marriage to a woman who was timid about the weather?

"Emily is recovering from an earache," her mother explained.

"I'm sorry to hear that." Immediately he set aside his doubts. Of course she shouldn't be out in the weather if she was not well.

He stayed only a short while. After a time, he simply ran out of conversation. Rising, he said, "I shall call for you tomorrow."

"Very well, milord." She smiled demurely.

Yes, he reflected as he placed his curly-brimmed beaver hat on his head, Emily was precisely what he wanted. She was a lady in every respect. The fact that she had nursed her late husband with solicitude until the time of his death added to his esteem for her. He was sure she would make a fine mother for his children.

Lady Marsh's small rout was a week after Priscilla performed her magic at the Lindham's. Priscilla and Mrs. Speers were late, due to the older woman dismissing the stablehand. He left abruptly, taking the keys to the stable with him so they couldn't get to the carriage. The other key was with a servant whom Mrs. Speers had sent off in search of exactly the right flower for Priscilla to wear that evening.

The servant was obviously having difficulty, perhaps owing to the exact shade of violet that Mrs. Speers had specified, and the man had not returned by the time they needed to leave. In the meantime,

Priscilla tore a large gash in her new white shawl. Her black one was soiled. In desperation, she pulled a hand-painted shawl from India from her trunk. She secretly thought its bright reds and yellows added some color to the drab lilac-colored dress, but she knew it was not in the way of the usual pale debutante colors.

Locked out of the stables, they were reduced to taking a hackney cab to the rout. Priscilla, at the last minute, grabbed a pin with Buddha painted on it and fastened it where the flower had been meant to go.

Mrs. Speers looked at the pin distractedly as the hackney jostled to a halt in front of Lady Marsh's. "It's a bit unusual, don't you think?"

"I like it," Priscilla said. "I bought it in Cairo when we were there."

The cab driver opened the door and stood waiting for his money. "I suppose it will do." Flustered, Mrs. Speers counted out the amount and hurried Priscilla toward the front door.

They were late enough that their entrance caused notice. Priscilla pulled her shawl tighter around her as eyes turned in their direction. The color riding high on her cheeks was very close to the red in her shawl. Her dark curls were tousled.

She heard an older lady comment that she looked more like a hoyden than a lady. However, none of the gentlemen seemed disposed to be so disapproving. If their expressions were any indication, a good number of the men were charmed by her flushed appearance.

Priscilla had only a vague impression of these opinions before she saw the earl. He was standing beside a slender, delicate-looking woman. As she watched, the woman said something to him, and he bent toward her with more attentiveness than he had ever accorded Priscilla.

Mrs. Speers nudged her. "Dear, let the man take your wrap."

Priscilla looked at the servant who stood with hand politely outstretched. "Oh, of course." She surrendered the brightly-colored shawl and moved forward into the room.

People nodded to her with friendly smiles. Those she knew by name spoke to her warmly. Alexandria, a young woman who was making her come-out, touched Priscilla's arm and smiled.

"What a lovely shawl you were wearing. So colorful. Where did you get it?"

"In Cairo."

Alexandria pulled a frown. "I wish Papa had gone abroad. All he's ever done is sit in Parliament and look after a few estates here in England. It's not at all glamorous."

Two other young debutantes crowded in close, agreeing morosely that they, too, had been denied exciting lives. One of the young ladies remarked, "You're very lucky, Priscilla. I should have liked above all things to grow up in India. Was it terribly dangerous?"

"Well, there was a man in a nearby village killed by a tiger last year," Priscilla said.

"How frightful!"

The music started, and men presented themselves to her for a dance. It was while she was doing a country set with Lord Massey that she noticed Lord Knole dancing with the delicate-looking woman.

"Who is that with the earl?" she asked casually when the movement of the dance brought her and her partner together again.

"Emily Simpson."

"I think I met her husband a short time ago."

"Couldn't have. She ain't got a husband. That is, she had one but he's dead. Has been three years now."

"Oh." Then Emily Simpson was out of mourning and eligible to wed again. Was that why Lord Knole was looking at her with such tender attention? Priscilla and Lord Massey danced down the set, moving closer to the earl.

Lord Knole smiled at his partner. Turning back to her own partner, Priscilla beamed with the intensity of a thousand candles. Then, laughing gaily at nothing at all, she danced by the earl.

Bemused but obviously gratified, Lord Massey returned a besotted grin.

"Such a lovely dance," she breathed.

"Yes." His gaze remained on her face.

Priscilla sneaked another look at the earl. His attention was no longer on Emily. He was looking at *her*. Good. With an expression as warm as she could generate, she moved forward to meet Lord Massey again. If the earl thought she could not charm men, he was sadly mistaken.

A few moments later, the dance ended. Lord Knole left the floor with Emily Simpson. Giles Wentworth showed up to claim Priscilla, looking pleased beyond all reasoning that he should have such an honor.

"I say, Miss Springton, that was a dashed good show you put on at the Lindham's. Don't mind telling you I'm fagged to death of listening to girls hammer on the pianoforte."

"I'm glad you liked it." She searched the crowd to see if Lord Knole and Emily Simpson were still together.

"Don't think there's anything about you I wouldn't like," he confided. With a voice full of woe, he added, "I'm afraid half the men in London feel that way, so I won't stand much chance. The *beau monde* is fascinated with you. We don't get many Indian princesses with such noble English blood here in London. You're an exotic bird."

The earl came into view, and Priscilla widened her smile at Giles. "How kind of you to say so." She wished she had her fan with her so that she could tap his wrist with it the way she had seen other ladies do. Not that she wished to make the earl jealous, but she wanted him to know that others did not find her wanting even if he did.

For the next two hours, she danced without stop. It was heady stuff being the center of attention, and Priscilla enjoyed every minute of it. She didn't care that the earl didn't ask her to dance. Well, not very much.

Chapter 7

The next day dawned gloomy with thunderclouds rumbling. Although no one braved the weather to call on Priscilla, several gentlemen sent notes and flowers.

It was an excellent opportunity to work on her painting, so she set up her easel in the little sitting room with the chintz curtains next to her bedroom. Geoffrey had become almost insistent about her finishing her work in progress. Yet even knowing he was anxious to have the picture, she found it difficult to concentrate.

As she mixed paints to achieve just the right shade of blue used in a picture she was copying from, she thought about last night. She had encouraged several men solely because Lord Knole had been present.

No one had called her to task for this, but she felt foolish. Why should she cast out wiles to a man simply to make another man wish he had taken an interest in her? Lord Knole had made it plain that she did not fulfill what he needed in a wife. Why could she not accept that?

With a start, she realized she had been so preoccupied with her thoughts, she had mixed the blue dangerously close to black. Making a face, she started over.

The door opened, and Maria stepped quietly in. "Will you need me this morning?"

"No, I shouldn't think so. It's a dreadful day to contemplate going out."

Maria nodded and was gone.

Perhaps Priscilla was looking for a distraction, but she thought there had been something secretive about the way Maria had acted. Rising, she went to the door and opened it to see the maid descending the back steps. Then Priscilla heard the back door open.

Good heavens, Maria was going out. Where would she be going on such a day? Now that Priscilla thought about it, the maid had seemed evasive in answering questions of late.

Hurrying to her room, she grabbed a brown pelisse. Flinging it over her shoulders, she went down the steps. She hadn't made a clear decision to follow her maid. She only knew that curiosity was drawing her in the same direction Maria had taken.

Out on the street, she saw the Indian woman moving briskly toward the west. Priscilla picked up her skirts and followed. She remained at a distance and just rounded a corner in time to see Maria climb into a hackney cab.

Priscilla looked around for a cab. She was not sure how a lady went about hailing one, but she was in luck. A big-bellied driver stopped beside her.

"Needin' a ride, miss?"

"Yes," she breathed thankfully. The scent of the chase was in her blood now, and she was determined that Maria not vanish.

"Where are you going?" the driver called back to her.

"I'm with that other cab." She pointed toward it. "I want to go wherever they go."

The driver shrugged. Priscilla opened the door for herself and climbed in. "Hurry."

He set off at a brisk pace, swerving to the left as he made a fast turn. A moment later Priscilla found herself sliding to the right. Shortly afterward, it was back to the left again. With the weather so bad and the streets bare of traffic, it was possible for the driver to keep up a good clip. He rounded corners and shot down straight stretches with alarming speed.

Her breakfast from two hours ago started to churn in her stomach and then to rise into her throat. She clung to the strap and concentrated on calming her queasiness. It was hopeless. The more the coach bucked and swayed, the more ill she became. Maria's destination ceased to matter to Priscilla. She only wanted to escape this wild ride.

Covering her mouth with one hand, she tugged the rope with the other.

The driver glanced back.

"I want to go back," she said weakly.

He didn't slow down. "But I've got 'em in sight."

"Back home," she repeated weakly, and clamped a hand firmly over her mouth.

He obeyed. He even diminished his speed, but she was too nauseated to fully appreciate this. When he came to a jolting halt in front of the place where he had picked her up, she directed him on down to Mrs. Speers's house. He stopped in front of it, and she reached feebly for the door, stepped out, and stood unsteadily on the sidewalk.

"Thank you," she murmured and turned to go into the house.

"You ain't paid me," the driver bellowed.

"I haven't any money with me. Wait here, I'll go inside and get some." The spirit was willing, but when she looked up at the dozen steps she had to mount to get into the house, the flesh faltered.

The fat driver mistook her hesitation for reluctance to pay him. His voice grew even more strident. "I'm not in the 'abit of givin' free rides, ma'am."

She shook her head, wanting to explain but afraid to take her hand away from her mouth.

Priscilla didn't see the earl walk up. But then, she was not in a state to notice much. All she knew was that he drew out his purse and paid enough to evoke a warm smile from the driver. Then the earl turned briskly to her. "Where have you been?"

"Out," she managed.

"I can see that," he snapped. "Out where?"

"Could we go inside?" she asked faintly. "I'm—I'm not feeling quite the thing."

He put a hand on her elbow. His touch felt rough, and she could feel his impatience, but she still leaned heavily against him. Once inside, she rushed to her room and was sick in the chamber pot. Feeling weak but better, she washed off her face, put a hand on the wall, and supported herself downstairs to the parlor.

She found the earl standing by the window. He dropped the curtain and turned when she entered.

"I'm better," she murmured, and tried for a smile.

"Sit down, Miss Springton," he said tersely.

She obeyed.

"I should like to hear why you were out in a hackney cab without a chaperone or a maid."

Priscilla didn't even consider telling him she was following her maid. It would be a betrayal to discuss Maria's wanderings until she had talked to the maid. Instead, Priscilla offered a lame, "I was bored and wished for something to do."

His expression hardened. "A lady does not go about by herself. If anyone had seen you in a hackney cab unescorted, it would have set tongues wagging."

Weak and intimidated by his glare, she said nothing.

"And while we are on the subject, you flirted shamelessly last night. I am trying to help you look like a pattern-card of respectability. I cannot hope to succeed if you cast out lures to every man who asks you to dance."

Unexpected tears stung at her eyes. Still feeling the effects of her recent carriage sickness, she blinked rapidly against the tears.

"Have you anything to say for yourself?" he demanded harshly.

"I think you're dreadful," she blurted, and fled up to her own room. There she slammed the door, threw herself on her bed, and cried.

Half an hour later, there was a tap on the door.

It was Lady Roseman.

Her ladyship must have seen the traces of tears, but she tactfully did not pry.

Instead, she removed her shawl and sat down on a chair. "I tire so easily these days," she murmured.

Priscilla looked from Lady Roseman's fuller face to the lump in her stomach. "I had no idea that you were . . . That is, I didn't know you were going to have a child."

"Indeed, I am," Lady Roseman said with a soft smile. "That's why I haven't been about in society," she added.

"Oh."

"A ridiculous custom, I think. Why shouldn't women who are breeding be seen out? After all, having children is a perfectly natural thing. Besides," she added with a laugh, "lying in can be dreadfully boring."

"I would have come to visit had I known you wanted entertainment."

Lady Roseman's smile deepened. "When would you have time to visit? Between drives in the park with the earl, magic performances at soirees, and receiving countless callers, I suspect you have precious little free time."

"It has been a bit hectic," Priscilla had to agree. Her gaze, quite without her wishing it, wandered back to the other woman's stomach. What did it feel like to be carrying a child? she wondered.

Lady Roseman, as if sensing the question, said quietly, "This is a strange time for me. Sometimes I feel quite heavy and ugly, and other times I feel very beautiful."

Not knowing how to reply, Priscilla said nothing.

"Well, we needn't talk only of me. Is there any particular man who has caught your eye?" Lady Roseman asked.

Priscilla shook her head.

"I thought a man might have inspired those tears," her ladyship pursued.

Priscilla pulled a face. "The earl was very unkind to me earlier."

"I see." After a pause, Lady Roseman added, "He, like any man, can be difficult. But he's not usually unkind. At least not on purpose. He—"

"He contradicts himself," Priscilla interrupted, and rose from the edge of the bed to pace. "He wants me to find a husband, and then he faults me for

97

casting out lures." She reached the end of the long room, whirled and retraced her steps. "I did nothing more than be friendly. I was certainly never improper."

"No, I'm sure you were not."

"I have had a number of callers, yet he finds fault with all of them."

"Indeed. How puzzling."

"Yes, especially since he is so anxious to see me married off." Priscilla paused at the window and looked out. For no reason at all, she recalled the way Emily Simpson had smiled at the earl last night.

When she turned back, Lady Roseman was frowning at her. "Priscilla, sometimes we develop tendres—form attachments, that is—toward men we think we dislike. What I'm trying to say is that you must not let yourself begin to care for the earl."

Priscilla blinked at her. "That is the most unlikely notion you could entertain. I am counting the days until someone offers for me, so that I never have to deal with him again."

"I hope you are," Lady Roseman said softly. "For you must know that he intends to make a completely proper alliance."

And she, Priscilla admitted to herself for the first time, was not good enough for him.

Lord Knole touched the perfect Oriental knot of his cravat and stepped down from his carriage. The party at the Branson's tonight was to be a small, very select affair. He was one of only a handful of the *ton* who had received an invitation.

In truth, he had little wish to be here. The morning's meeting with Priscilla weighed on his mind. She had had no business being out unescorted, and he had been perfectly right to tell her so. But he had seen the quick glitter of tears in her eyes before she ran from the room. That memory bothered him as he stepped into the paneled entryway.

"Good evening, Robert."

"Good evening, Lady Branson." His hostess had been an acknowledged beauty in her youth. Even at five-and-thirty, she was a striking woman. She wore pearl combs in her dark red hair, but it was the brightly colored shawl around her shoulders that caught his eye.

She noticed his gaze and laughed. "Do you like it? My maid was out all day searching for one. They aren't easy to find, you know."

"It's unusual," he said tactfully.

Lady Branson extended her arm, and he put his hand on her elbow, escorting her into a room with tracery work on the ceiling, and windows of heavy leaded glass. A dozen women were present and as many men. Half the women clung to shawls of Indian design. Hadn't Priscilla worn something like that the other night?

Lady Jersey floated up to him. "I'm very disappointed in you, Robert."

"I cannot think why."

She tossed her head. "Don't come the innocent with me. You have not introduced me to your ward. The whole of the town is talking about her. It makes me feel quite gauche not to have met her."

Lord Knole was taken aback. The very notion that Lady Jersey, the queen of London society, would want to meet Priscilla Springton startled him. "She's only been in London a short time," he said mildly.

"Long enough to have started a rage in Indian shawls," Sally Jersey noted tartly. "And I am here with my white lace shawl. Really, Robert, it makes me look ridiculous."

Lady Jersey practically ruled polite society. Her rooms in the upstairs of Almack's were the place to see and be seen. It mattered not a whit that she served only stale cakes and insipid punch. Anyone with pretensions to acceptability aspired to vouchers to those hallowed rooms. That Priscilla had come to Lady Jersey's attention surprised the earl.

He bestowed his most charming smile. "It was never my intention to exclude you from an introduction. I should be pleased to bring her to your house any morning that is convenient for you."

"Tomorrow," she said promptly.

"Of course."

She sailed away. Bemused, Lord Knole moved slowly toward the corner where Emily sat with her mother and another dowager on Sheraton chairs. His thoughts were on the encounter he had just had. For Lady Jersey to acknowledge the existence of someone not of the *ton* was unusual. For her to ask to meet that person was nothing short of astonishing.

Emily smiled demurely up at him.

He bowed to all three of the ladies, then addressed himself to the younger woman, "You are looking very lovely this evening." Her delicate blue silk made her look even more dainty.

"Thank you," she said sweetly.

"I'm glad the weather has improved. It was most unpleasant this morning."

"It was indeed." She continued to watch him pleasantly, but offered no further conversation. After a few moments, he moved away. He didn't really mind that she had so little to say. Surely if one were to spend more time with her, she would begin to converse more.

Lord Knole circulated among the guests.

A short time later, Emily was prevailed upon to sing something for the group. She chose a ballad and sang it in a beautiful voice. The earl had always enjoyed her singing, yet for some reason, he found himself fidgeting. He even dipped his hand into his pocket to look at his watch.

He had felt this restlessness whose source he could not identify more and more of late. He could not imagine its cause. He would leave early tonight, he decided, and go to White's. A game of faro would relax him.

The following morning when Maria appeared to help with her toilette, Priscilla said directly, "I was surprised to see you leave yesterday."

The maid looked startled.

"I don't wish you to think that I was spying on you, but I am curious about where you went."

"I wanted to see something of the city, miss," Maria replied quietly.

"Oh." Priscilla paused. She would not have chosen such an unpleasant day for sight-seeing, but if her maid wished to do so, Priscilla could scarcely reprimand her. Maria had not precisely said that she was leaving the house, but she had asked if she would be needed. Deciding not to make a mountain out of a molehill, Priscilla dropped the subject.

Instead she finished dressing and then began painting. Geoffrey had called yesterday afternoon and had come perilously close to anger when she told him she was not finished with the painting.

"I'm only doing it as a favor," she had reminded him.

101

"I told you I will pay you. Besides, when you tell me you will have it done on a certain day, I expect you to keep your word."

She *had* given him a date when she expected to be finished, Priscilla reflected. Well, she would complete this painting and then refuse to do any more. She was beginning to dislike Geoffrey, but he *was* Mrs. Speers's nephew, so she could scarcely be rude to him.

As she was dipping the brush into the paint pot, Esther appeared with a letter. Priscilla recognized her father's handwriting and eagerly tore the envelope open. Her enthusiasm dimmed with the first lines.

"Child, when is the wedding to be?"

Sinking onto the bed, she continued reading as the maid quietly left the room. The rest of the page was filled with questions very like the first one. In her father's usual forthright way, he wanted things to proceed rapidly, and he wanted to be kept apprised of all results. While Priscilla had written several letters home since arriving in London, she had carefully skirted the issue of a betrothal to the earl.

Sighing, she kicked at the side of the bed with slippered feet. She would have to write to her father and tell him the earl did not wish to marry her.

She walked to the burled maple writing desk and pulled out a sheet of paper. After mending a pen and arranging the paper just so on the desk, she tried to write. The first attempt was unsuccessful. She tried again.

It was futile. The pile of discarded paper slowly grew to a mound at the floor by her feet. She could find no way to convince her father in a letter that things were not going to be the way he had envisioned them.

"This is hopeless," she murmured, and went in search of Mrs. Speers. She found her chaperone in the dining room wiping smudges of chocolate off her fingers and avidly reading a gothic novel.

"I must go to Kent for a visit." Priscilla braced herself for an argument.

"Very well." Mrs. Speers flipped to the next page.

Priscilla blinked. "Then you don't object?"

"Not in the least," the older woman said airily. "I've always liked Kent."

Priscilla smiled her relief. "I shan't be gone more than a week. I wouldn't go at all if it were not absolutely necessary," she added.

"Of course, dear." With an absent pat on Priscilla's cheek, Mrs. Speers put another chocolate into her mouth and continued reading.

Priscilla went upstairs to pack. Maria helped her, but she seemed to be moving slowly. Impatient, Priscilla summoned Esther.

By one in the afternoon everything was prepared. There seemed no reason to wait until the morning to leave. Consequently, the carriage was loaded, and Priscilla and Esther headed for Kent.

As the carriage jolted southward, Priscilla rehearsed what she would say to her father once she was face to face with him.

Lord Knole had several pressing things he should be attending to today. His estate manager from Sussex had come up, and the earl needed to confer with him. Tattersall's was holding a horse for his inspection. Sir Owen Phillips wished to consult with him over a boys' charity home to which the earl contributed.

Instead, however, he found himself mounting the steps to Mrs. Speers's house. Lady Jersey had said she wished to meet Priscilla, and that amounted to a royal summons. It was a singular honor for a girl with no notable family lineage to meet Lady Jersey.

A footman opened the door, and the earl was shown into the parlor. A moment later Mrs. Speers appeared. Judging from her rumpled skirts, she had just arisen from a nap.

She greeted him with the flirtatiousness of a schoolgirl, coyly offering him her hand. "How pleasant to see you, milord."

"It's always a pleasure to see you, Mrs. Speers." He released her hand. Good lord, his fingers felt sticky.

"It bids fair to being a sunny day."

"Yes." He glanced at his watch fob. If they were quick he could take Priscilla to meet Lady Jersey and still see Sir Owens. "Please tell Miss Springton to put on her finest dress. I wish to take her to meet Lady Jersey."

"That's quite impossible."

"I should have thought so myself, but her ladyship has requested a meeting. Please summon Pris—Miss Springton." He pivoted away on one shiny boot.

Mrs. Speers continued to stand unmoving.

He turned back to her. "Is there a problem?"

"Priscilla has gone to Kent."

The earl stared. He surely had not heard correctly. "Gone to Kent?"

"Not for good," she hastened to assure him. "Only for a visit."

"My good woman," he said carefully, unconsciously flicking his riding crop against his thigh,

104

"surely you don't mean to say that Miss Springton has left London at the height of the Season."

"I'm afraid she has."

"Why?"

"I didn't think to ask her."

How had he ever thought Mrs. Speers would be a competent chaperone? She had clearly lost whatever brains her maker had given her. The earl flicked the riding crop faster. "When did she leave?" He plotted mentally. He could send riders after her if she had not been gone too long.

The older woman frowned. "I cannot recall."

The earl bit back an angry epithet and tried again. "When will she return?"

"Oh," she smiled, clearly pleased to be asked something for which she had the answer, "in a week."

The earl looked toward the ceiling. Sally Jersey was waiting to meet Priscilla, and the mindless chit was on her way to Kent. And here stood Mrs. Speers, a woman being paid quite well to supervise Priscilla's introduction into society, and she hadn't yet given a sensible answer to any question he asked her.

"You are to write her a letter and send it by special messenger. Tell her she is to return immediately. No," he said sharply, "I shall take care of the matter myself. In the future, you are to make no decisions concerning Miss Springton without consulting me."

"Yes, milord," she agreed with a sunny smile.

Lord Knole stalked out the door and back to his carriage.

Priscilla's parents were pleased beyond measure to see her. After engulfing her in a fierce hug, her father steered her toward the house.

105

"I've built an aviary. You must see it."

"Let the child wash off the travel dust first," her mother objected.

"She doesn't mind a paltry thing like a bit of dust," Mr. Springton scoffed, still herding her into the house and down a hallway. "You should see all the birds I've got. Beautiful birds. Some can even speak."

Her mother hurried along in their wake, tattling, "He's teaching them to say improper things."

They ended up in a room with a vaulted ceiling. Grills covered the windows. Birds of every description clung to perches, plucked grain from the floor, and swooped about in the air. The sound of chirping, screeching, and cooing nearly drowned out conversation.

"Don't just stand there, child. Close the door or they'll get out. Come over here and see my prize."

Priscilla followed her father to a corner of the hall. The jet black bird really could talk. For a few moments she listened politely. But the sound of its shrill "Hello, hello!" grew monotonous.

"That's wonderful, Papa. Could we go somewhere to talk?"

He cupped his hand around his ear. "What?"

"That's wonderful," she shouted.

"It can say other things, too."

"Victor," his wife said warningly. Turning to Priscilla, she continued, "We're so glad you've come, child. We've missed you."

"I've missed you, too, Mama." Priscilla gave her mother an impulsive hug, then drew in a deep breath. She was here now; she might as well get it over with. "Papa, there's something I have to tell you."

106

Her father's fond gaze remained on the bird. "He doesn't say too much now, but with a little training, he'll learn hundreds of words. Maybe thousands!"

Taking his hand gently, Priscilla pulled him out of the room. Her mother followed. "I'm glad to see both of you, but I didn't come all this way for a visit. I have something to tell you."

The severity of her tone must have conveyed itself, for her mother frowned and her father looked doubtful. "Not bad news, I hope," he said.

"I'm not going to marry the earl." There, she had said it. Expelling her pent-up breath, she looked from one of her parents to the other.

Their expressions were blank.

"Why not?" her father asked.

"Because he doesn't wish to marry me."

"Blast him. Of course he will marry you. He owes it to me. Told me himself he was indebted to me for saving his father's life."

Priscilla felt hot with embarrassment. There had clearly never been any real plans for her to marry the earl; only those laid in her father's mind.

"I've half a mind to call him out. Yes, that's what I shall do. Where are my pistols, madame? If the scoundrel thinks to throw my daughter over, I shall dispatch him on his merry way to the next world."

"Victor, you're talking nonsense," Mrs. Springton said.

Priscilla's father's anger subsided as quickly as it had come. He looked plaintively at his daughter. "Why won't he marry you? You've a dowry far beyond that of other girls. Doesn't he know I'm as rich as Croesus?"

"He wants someone of his own class," Priscilla said quietly.

Her father looked pained.

"But there are other men in London," she added in a rush. "Some of them like me very well indeed. I shouldn't be surprised if I couldn't marry someone just as well to pass as the earl." Wanting to erase the unhappiness on her father's face, she kept talking, gathering speed and neglecting truth. "I'm fond of two particular gentlemen. I should be happier being a wife to either of them as I would be being wed to Lord Knole."

"You really like someone better?" her mother asked tentatively.

"Yes! And London is wondrous fun. I can scarcely wait to return."

A look of relief crossed her mother's face. Even her father looked somewhat mollified.

"Well, if you're certain. Otherwise, I shall come to London and deal with the man myself."

"No, that's not necessary."

Three days later, Priscilla left to return to London. Due to a horse throwing a shoe and a bit of bad luck with directions, the messenger that Lord Knole had sent after Priscilla did not reach the house until after she had departed. The weary man was somewhat surprised when Mr. Springton threw him bodily out of the house.

Chapter 8

"Lord Knole is here and wishes to see you."

Priscilla laid aside her brushes, took off her apron, and smoothed the skirts of her blue muslin gown before proceeding down the steps.

She had not seen or spoken with the earl since returning from Kent yesterday. Thoughts of him had flashed through her mind more frequently than she cared to admit. The memory of their last conversation was fresh enough in her mind that she ought to dread seeing him. Yet her steps were brisk and eager as she started toward the parlor.

There she found the earl pacing. His long steps showed off the tight muscles in his calves. Absurdly she noted the length of his eyelashes as she greeted him.

He looked at her a moment in silence. "I've a mind to ring a peal over your head, but Lady Roseman says that would not serve. I daresay she is right," he continued ruefully. "What's done is done even if you did miss the opportunity to meet Lady Jersey."

Priscilla tilted her head to the side quizzically. "I beg your pardon, milord?"

"Never mind." A wry smile hooked the corners of his mouth upward. "Sit down, Priscilla."

Until now she had been Miss Springton. She didn't know if the move to her given name was a good sign or a bad one. She took a place on the settee and waited.

The earl sat across from her in a wing chair with a back high enough to cast part of his face in shadows. "It has come to my attention—or rather Lady Roseman has brought it to my attention that a young woman's first Season can be a difficult time. When that young lady leaves without warning to return to her home, it creates a goodly number of problems. It also makes one wonder if she is unhappy." He paused, then seemed to force himself to proceed. "*Are* you unhappy, Priscilla?"

She blinked at the question. It was almost easier when he was gruff. At least she could deal with that. But his look of confusion and the concern with which he had put the question caught her off guard. "I-I don't know," she stammered.

"Why did you go home?"

Priscilla lowered her eyes. When the pause grew too long, she forced herself to say, "I had to talk to my parents."

"Why?"

She glanced toward the window. Wasn't it bad enough that he had said he didn't wish to marry her? To tell him she had made the trip to Kent to make that fact known to her parents only added to her humiliation.

He cleared his throat. "Has any man been untoward in his attentions?"

"I don't know what you mean."

"Has anyone tried to take liberties? To kiss you or force his attentions on you?"

110

The meaning of his carefully-chosen words hit her, and she flushed. "No. Definitely not."

He seemed to relax. "Then perhaps you are dissatisfied with Mrs. Speers. You needn't worry; I mean to change that. I shall make arrangements for you to have another chaperone."

She absorbed this news slowly. "Leave Mrs. Speers?"

"Yes. It is now possible for you to have someone more—suitable."

Priscilla shook her head with enough conviction to send the soft curls around her forehead dancing. "No, I want to stay here. I like it here." Besides, Mrs. Speers needed the money.

"But you do not *have* to stay," he explained patiently. "There are other places to live and other women willing to introduce you."

"Where were they before?" she asked bluntly.

That brought him to halt. He examined the roses patterned into the rug before saying, "To be perfectly frank, you are more acceptable as a charge now than you were a few weeks ago."

"I don't wish to live with people who wouldn't trouble themselves with me before." Pride made her words more strident. "Merely because I've become acceptable to *them* does not mean they have become so to *me*."

Something like admiration lit in his eyes momentarily. "I might feel the same way," he admitted in a voice so low she had to strain to hear him. In a louder voice, he continued, "At any rate, there's little those women can do to enhance your reputation now." Reaching into his pocket, he extracted an envelope. "This came while you were gone. It contains a voucher to Almack's."

111

She took the envelope, fingering it silently. "This is good, isn't it?"

He smiled. "Most women would consider it so."

Priscilla had heard much about the rooms of Almack's. She had even envied those who attended the soirees held there, yet now that she was being included in that select circle, a feeling of insecurity amounting to panic seized her. "You *will* go with me, won't you?" she demanded.

"Yes."

"And stand by my side when I'm introduced to the patronesses," she pressed.

"Yes, of course."

"And help me remember their names." Frowning, she tried to recall them. "Let me see—there's a Russian countess. Whatever is her name? And there's—" She paused at the sound of his low chuckle. Stung, she lifted her chin. "You may find it diverting, but I assure you it is very serious business to me."

That seemed to amuse him further.

"Have you never been frightened of anything?" she challenged.

The laughter died away. "I've feared losing someone."

Priscilla hesitated, sensing the change of atmosphere. "Your wife?" she asked tentatively.

"Yes."

A wiser woman might have let the subject go, but something compelled Priscilla to say, "I know it can be very hard to have someone or something taken away. My loss does not compare with yours, but I still recall the desolation I felt when we left India. It was the only life I had known, and suddenly I was being taken to a strange land to live out the rest of my days."

He nodded in understanding.

Priscilla wondered where the conversation might have gone had not Mrs. Speers chosen that moment to arrive. She came bustling through the door murmuring her greetings to the earl and fussing with her shawl.

A short time later the earl left.

That evening Lord Knole sat in Lady Margaret Capulet's drawing room. He was dressed in a buff-colored coat; sleek white unmentionables showed his masculine legs to good advantage. From his seat in the fourth row, he watched a young woman attempt a card trick.

In the past few days, pianofortes and harps all over London had gathered dust while young ladies turned their dubious talents to cards. When a debutante was called upon to entertain at a soiree these days, like as not, she would produce a deck of cards.

The young lady performing at the moment, a Miss Amanda Farley, had just succeeded in dropping the cards a second time. Two young swains in the front row again leapt to their feet to help pick them up. At other times the earl might have been impatient, but tonight he felt calm. He had since speaking with Priscilla earlier today.

The card trick continued. Amanda asked a man in the audience to pick a card. He did.

"What card did you choose, sir?"

"The king of spades."

"That's precisely the card I have in my pocket." She produced the card with a flourish. It turned out to be the three of hearts.

The forgiving audience applauded anyway, and Miss Farley left the stage looking less mortified than she might have done.

Three more young ladies entertained with cards. None had the the smooth, sure deftness of Priscilla, Lord Knole observed.

"Milord."

He looked up with a start to see Emily Simpson bending toward him. The entertainment was over, and around him people were rising.

"Is it time for refreshments already?"

"Yes."

He was not hungry, but he joined the others anyway, absently putting food on his plate. Emily, he noticed, kept darting questioning looks at him. He ought to pay more attention to her, he reflected guiltily. He *was* courting her.

In fact, it was time he moved into a more intense phase of courting.

As soon as they had finished eating, he took her arm and steered her toward the French doors that opened out onto a balcony. "Why don't we go outside for a breath of air?" he suggested urbanely.

Emily allowed herself to be led outside. She even followed him to the dark corner of the balcony near the stone steps that led down to a lower terrace.

"You're looking very lovely tonight," he murmured as he bent toward her.

She allowed him a chaste kiss on her cheek. Encouraged, he put his arms around her, pulled her against him, and dipped his head again. This time he kissed her mouth.

Emily wrenched out of his grasp. "Sir, you're forgetting yourself!"

The earl straightened. "I humbly beg your pardon. We shall return to the party immediately."

"I think we should," she agreed huffily.

Like a perfect gentleman, he led her back inside. Throughout the rest of the evening, the earl acted with complete propriety toward Emily. There was nothing in his manner to indicate that a small doubt had crept into his mind. Yet he had enough experience with women to know when one was being coy or virtuous. Emily, he realized, had been neither. She simply did not like to kiss. What was more, he suspected there were other, more intimate, pleasures of the senses that she would not find to her liking. It was a daunting thought for a prospective bridegroom.

"I'm sorry I haven't finished your painting, Geoffrey. I simply have not had the time." Priscilla didn't know why talking to Mrs. Speers's nephew made her so nervous these days. She had been putting off telling him that work on the painting was progressing slowly. Twice she had had to start over on the project due to a bad mixture of colors.

He glared at her.

The two of them were on the small terrace behind Mrs. Speers's house.

"You must *make* time," he grumbled.

Exasperation got the better of her. "Geoffrey, pray remember I am doing this as a favor."

"I've promised it to someone," he returned testily.

"Then you shall have to explain to that person that—"

"Finish it," he said tightly.

Priscilla stared at him. Whatever was the matter with him? He had been charming when she first met him. Now his manner was almost threatening.

Behind her, the door opened and Mrs. Speers appeared. The older woman was full of chatter about the weather and the lovely flowers. She remained wholly ignorant of the tension between her nephew and Priscilla.

Priscilla took the first opportunity to escape. Being away from Geoffrey made her braver than she had felt in his presence. On the way up the stairs, she muttered to herself, "If he thinks he can order me about, he is sadly mistaken. I should have told him—" Opening her door, she broke off, startled to see her maid asleep in a chair in the corner of the room.

"Maria," she said.

No response.

She called in a louder voice.

The maid sat bolt upright.

"Are you ill?" Priscilla asked.

"No, only tired." She rose quickly and smoothed her dark hair. "I'm terribly sorry."

Priscilla stopped her from leaving. "Is anything amiss?"

"No, nothing," the maid replied quickly. "I sat down for but a moment, and I was asleep. It won't happen again," she continued apologetically.

Priscilla was still worried. "Are you getting enough sleep at night?"

"Oh, yes, miss." She looked longingly toward the door. "Was there anything more?"

There was little else for Priscilla to say. "No, you may go."

The maid slipped out the door.

Not two seconds later, a knock sounded, and Mrs. Speers sailed in. "A letter for you, dear. By the handwriting, I judge it to be from a man." She waited unabashedly for Priscilla to read the missive.

Priscilla opened it and scanned it absently, still distracted by thoughts of Maria.

Mrs. Speers peered over Priscilla's shoulder. "What does he say?"

"It's a poem." Another one, she thought wearily. Of late she had received a goodly number of poems.

"How lovely!"

Priscilla found it nothing of the sort. The poetry she had received thus far was always long and tedious. If the poet must compare her to something, surely he could be more original than a flower. Yet here was another poem comparing her hair to soft petals and her walk to a stem moving in the breeze.

Mrs. Speers patted her cheek. "You are quite a success. You have half of London at your feet."

Somehow, that knowledge was not satisfying. She didn't want to be the center of attention today. And she didn't wish to sit in the parlor with a smile pressed on her face while men vied for her attention. At the moment, she wanted to be by herself.

"I believe I shall go in search of a new bonnet," she said abruptly.

"Now? Callers shall be arriving at any moment! You cannot leave now."

"I simply must have a new bonnet. You can entertain them. I'll take a maid with me." Without waiting for a reply, Priscilla grabbed her pelisse and rushed down the stairs.

The English maid Esther seemed startled at being summoned in such a ramshackle fashion, but she came quickly enough.

A short time later they alighted at Burlington Arcade. Priscilla visited three millinery shops before boredom with trying on hats overcame her. She was not, however, ready to go back. Strolling along the arcade, she glanced into several of the windows.

One shop sold fine silver. Another offered kid

gloves as soft and supple as silk. Unintrigued, she continued walking.

Outside an art shop she halted and gazed raptly through the window. The pictures inside were clearly not the efforts of novices. Beautiful master-pieces crowded the small window. She was drawn inside the shop like metal shavings to a magnet. Her maid followed.

The balding man who came forward to greet her was stiff with dignity.

"I wanted to look at your paintings." Shyly, she confided, "I paint."

He sniffed. "These, my dear lady, are not merely 'paintings.' They are the works of great artists."

Priscilla wished she had kept her foolish tongue in her head. "I shall look," she informed him with a belated attempt at hauteur.

He retreated without comment.

Priscilla did look, taking her time at a portrait of a young girl done by Turner. Then she studied a Rubens of a plump lady with very few clothes. She was too fascinated by the techniques of the artist to blush at the subject. And then she noted a Rey-nolds just like the one she had painted for Geoffrey.

She halted so quickly that she almost fell for-ward. The brush strokes of the Reynolds looked fa-miliar. She bent closer, and a gasp escaped her. This was no Reynolds; this was *her* painting.

The shopkeeper returned. "Is there a problem?"

Agitated, she whirled to face him. "Where did you get this painting?"

He drew himself up stiffly. "I do not divulge my sources."

"Why?"

"Because my transactions and what I pay for art are strictly confidential."

118

She stared with wide eyes. "You *bought* this painting from someone?"

"Naturally." His manner had grown even cooler.

Stunned, Priscilla moved woodenly toward the door. The painting had an outrageous price tag hanging discreetly beside it. The shopkeeper would make a great deal of money when it sold. Someone else had surely made a handsome sum by selling the painting to the shop.

That someone, she realized with horror, was Geoffrey Speers. He was passing her copies off as originals. No wonder he had been so insistent that she finish the one in progress. He needed the money it would bring. How could she have been so foolishly naive as to think he was giving them to friends?

A far more scary question was: What was she going to do now?

"Are we returning home?" the maid asked in her starched English accent.

Priscilla looked up to discover that she was seated in the carriage. She didn't even remember being handed in. All she could think about was the picture in the shop. How many other shops around town were also selling fake copies of Reynolds? *Her* fakes?

"Yes," she said a bit desperately. "Home." Instead of Mrs. Speers's little house, however, she pined for the cool, low house in India. If only she could escape there, she would be safe.

Throughout the drive home, she worried what to do next. She could not go to Mrs. Speers and tell her the truth: Geoffrey, blackguard that he was, was her chaperone's nephew, and she would be bound to defend him. Who could Priscilla turn to?

The earl? A chill ran up her arm at the thought of how he would react. No, she could never turn to him. She must not even let him find out what she had done. The only thing he cared about was seeing her married off. If it became known that she had forged paintings, surely it would ruin any chance of her making a suitable alliance.

So what was she to do?

Lord Knole was in his stables when word was sent that Sir Trevor wished to speak to him.

"What the devil can he want?" he muttered crossly.

He returned to his study to find the baronet waiting patiently. Trevor Kingsford was a kindly man considerably older than the earl. Most of the older man's time was spent in scholarly research of the writer Marlowe.

The earl entered his study, and the two men exchanged brief pleasantries. Questions were asked concerning family members, and the topic of the weather was glanced upon. The whole of the time, Lord Knole pondered the real purpose of the visit.

Finally, the baronet cleared his throat. "I believe you are Miss Priscilla Springton's guardian?"

"After a fashion."

"I wish to make her my wife."

It was the earl's turn to clear his throat. The baronet was well off financially. In fact, he possessed more than the earl had dared hope for when he agreed to bring Priscilla to London. So why was he hesitating?

"I am, of course, prepared to have my solicitor discuss my finances in depth with your solicitor. But I promise you that I can provide a proper home for the lady and give her a generous allowance."

"Yes, of course." Lord Knole fiddled with papers on his desk. Why not say yes? Instead he heard

120

himself saying, "Miss Springton has lived abroad most of her life and has not had a chance to learn all of our ways yet. Perhaps it is a bit soon to think of marriage."

"I am willing to instruct her," the older man said equably. "I realize, of course, that she must be agreeable to the match, but I fancy she likes me tolerably well."

The earl had always considered "liking someone tolerably well" a solid foundation for a marriage. Suddenly, however, it seemed not enough. "That's all very well, but her heart must be truly engaged before she could think of marrying."

The baronet looked at Lord Knole as if he'd taken leave of his senses. "She doesn't seem the type whose mind is full of romances from penny novels."

"No, of course not. She's a sensible girl, but she is very firm about wanting to be certain of her heart before marrying." If the men at White's could hear him, the earl reflected, they would lay wagers he had lost his senses. Yet here he was prepared to turn down a perfectly good offer. Why? It seemed certain that someone else would offer for Priscilla, but why wait? If he were to accept the baronet, the matter would be closed, and he would be absolved of all responsibility.

The baronet rose. "I shall give you time to consider my proposal. And to discuss it with the lady. I shall await your answer."

"Of course."

If he were seriously considering the proposal, Lord Knole reflected as the door closed behind his visitor, he would have discussed Priscilla's family circumstances. The fact that she was accepted in such places as Almack's had enhanced her social consequence, but she was not of the nobility. Any man who was seriously considering Priscilla as a wife would have to have the real facts laid out for him.

The earl could think of plenty of instances when peers had married beneath their station. There were, of course, an equal number of cases when members of the nobility had picked wives solely on the basis of lineage. Each man must make his own choice.

When the time came, Lord Knole would give an eligible suitor all the facts with which to make that choice. But there was no rush, was there? It might transpire that Priscilla had no interest in marrying the baronet, and then what would have been the point of laying out all the facts about her?

Chapter 9

The next three days were torturous for Priscilla. She longed for someone to confide in but could think of no one. Mrs. Speers was out of the question because of her relationship with Geoffrey. She didn't really know Lady Roseman well enough. Besides, in her delicate condition, Priscilla had no business taking problems to her.

She had considered purchasing the pictures and destroying them. But she didn't know how many were out there or where they were.

It was becoming clearer and clearer that she was going to have to deal with Geoffrey herself. He was the only one who could help her. She had heard rumors of his gambling and that he was always short of funds. If she offered him money, he would surely tell her where the pictures were so that she could buy them back. That would entail asking her father for an enormous amount of money. She would, of course, have to tell her father what was wrong. But until it was absolutely necessary, she didn't want to inform her parents. It would only cause them worry and grief.

For the past three days, Priscilla had carefully avoided the earl. Her instinct told her it would be the wisest course not to be around him. He seemed perfectly capable of deducing that something was bothering her, and she had no wish to answer any questions.

Of far greater weight was her fear of what would happen to her if it became known she had participated in this crime. Visions of gaol swept away her appetite. For three days she barely touched her food. Painting, of course, was out of the question. She devoted every minute of her time to worrying.

She was pacing in her room on the afternoon of the Wilmett's grand ball. Mrs. Speers bustled about in the background looking for a mislaid reticule, popping chocolates into her mouth, and insisting that Priscilla wear the green silk rather than the hitherto-agreed-upon pink.

"As you wish," Priscilla murmured passively.

"You've been acting very quiet of late," her chaperone noted. "I hope you're not ill."

"No, I feel fine. It's all the excitement." Priscilla managed a weak smile. She was going to have to make an effort to appear more normal. If even Mrs. Speers noticed that something was wrong, others were bound to.

"A Season is a bit overwhelming. Care for a chocolate? No? Perhaps later."

"Perhaps." Priscilla sat in front of the mirror. Esther began arranging her hair with silent deftness. Priscilla had been calling on the English maid more of late, thus allowing Maria more time to rest. Maria insisted she was fine, but Priscilla thought she looked tired.

Staring bleakly at her reflection in the mirror, Priscilla dreaded seeing Lord Knole that evening. How could she hope to be around him and not have him suspect something?

She could not help recalling their last conversation when she had shared with him her desolation at coming to England and he had talked about the loss of his wife. For a few moments, they had reached beyond the barriers of politeness and communicated to each other as real friends. Yet still she did not feel she could go to him with her problem. Partly, she was too embarrassed; partly, she feared how much it would hurt her if he refused to help.

Esther stepped back to silently survey her handiwork. Mrs. Speers was effusive. "Don't you look a picture with those dark curls dancing and the color high on your cheeks. That dress fits you to perfection. Such a lovely, slender figure you have. I had a figure exactly like that when I was younger. But you must not look so glum. Smile, pet."

Priscilla tried.

Mrs. Speers handed her a white shawl with silver embroidery and placed her reticule in her hand. Priscilla started toward the staircase. As she descended, she heard the front door open and saw the earl stride into the entryway below. The crown of his curly-brimmed beaver hat lifted until he was looking up at her.

He nodded slowly, as if his approval were being torn from him against his wishes. "Good evening, Priscilla."

"Good evening, milord." The knot in her stomach clenched tighter as she stepped off the last riser and stood before him.

"The poor dear is nervous," Mrs. Speers said from behind her. "She hasn't even had any appetite."

He turned a kind smile on her. "You needn't worry. It's true it is a large affair, but you will know dozens of people there."

125

She nodded without enthusiasm.

"You must save me a dance."

"Where *did* I put my reticule?" Mrs. Speers wondered aloud.

After a brief search for the missing reticule, the earl escorted the two women out to his waiting carriage. He gave the command, and they started toward the Wilmett's house.

"Are you still painting?" the earl enquired politely.

She felt chilled by the question. "Not much." She swallowed painfully. "Why do you ask?"

The capes of his many-tiered greatcoat lifted with his casual shrug. "No reason. I was merely making conversation."

Priscilla thought of the painting hanging in the gallery in Burlington Arcade and wondered again what were the consequences in England of forging paintings. In India people were hanged for far lesser offenses. She stared at the bobbing light on the side of the carriage as the enormity of that sank in.

Why had the earl brought up the subject of her painting? Did he know something?

She ventured a glance in his direction. The chiseled, immobile lines of his face revealed nothing. Then he glanced toward her and a small smile touched the corners of his mouth. "You are nervous. I can feel the tension."

"I shall be fine once we get there," she said in a bright, false voice.

"Of course you will," Mrs. Speers agreed, and patted her hand.

At length they arrived at the Wilmett's baroque mansion. Priscilla was thankful for the breath of cool night air on her cheeks as the earl handed her out of the carriage.

Beside her, Mrs. Speers talked happily. Her words covered the silence as the three of them mounted the marble steps. Halfway up the steps, Priscilla glanced toward the earl and saw him studying her narrowly. Quickly she looked away.

Quite aside from the earl—the lights, the music, the scent of perfume wafting out through the doors all served to make her uneasy. She was walking into a room filled with hundreds of people. If but one of them knew what she had done, she was lost. And, of course, Geoffrey *did* know. Would he be present? He had not yet been invited to any event she had attended, but that did not prevent her from worrying that tonight might be different.

"Such a press of people," Mrs. Speers said. "Wherever shall we find a place to sit?"

It proved to be a moot point for someone asked Priscilla to dance immediately. As she walked out onto the dance floor, she barely glanced at her partner.

She passed the next few hours in a daze. She danced, drank ratifia, and listened numbly to dozens of people talk. She was miserable wondering what was going to happen to her.

She was standing amidst a group of people, hearing nothing, and conscious only of the ache inside her, when her gaze wandered toward the earl. He stood taller than the men around him, and he looked strong and capable. She felt a surge of longing. Maybe she was wrong not to confide in him.

Then her gaze fell on the beautiful woman standing beside him, and her senses returned. Lord Knole's interest was in Emily Simpson. She had heard the betting was six to one at White's that the pair would wed. Why should the earl trouble himself with her problems when he had his own concerns to attend to?

Suddenly realizing that someone was speaking to her, she glanced toward the tall man bending eagerly toward her.

"I believe I have this dance," he said.

"Yes, of course."

It was two hours later when the earl came up to her and bowed. "May I have this dance?"

She couldn't bring herself to meet his gaze. "Thank you, but I have a partner."

"The next one then."

"I'm sorry, but I'm engaged for the rest of the dances."

"Then someone will be disappointed, won't he?" the earl said, and drew her firmly out onto the floor.

It was a waltz.

Nerves made her lash out at him. "Surely your obligation to my father does not extend so far that you must stand up with me for a dance."

He looked coolly down at her. "No, it does not. I rather thought I would enjoy holding you in my arms and watching you smile up at me the way I've seen you smile at other men."

She was speechless. Finally, she managed to sputter, "You have no right to speak that way to me."

"Of course not. You may bestow your smiles wherever you like. You did, however, promise to save me a dance, and I am taking it."

Priscilla heard a cruelness in his words that she had never detected there before. It was as if he meant to hurt her. At that moment she realized how truly alone she was. She could never turn to him for help. His feelings for her had so far diminished that he now actually disliked her.

128

* * *

Lord Knole had his beaver hat on his head, his blue superfine coat on his shoulders, and his snow-white unmentionables on his legs when he knocked at Emily Simpson's door the day after the Wilmett's ball. He also carried a large diamond-and-emerald ring in his pocket.

He was going to declare himself to Emily and ask her to marry him. It was a well-thought-out decision which took into account her social standing and her quiet and biddable ways. He did not look too closely into the fact he was making the offer the day after the Wilmett's ball, following a tense exchange with Priscilla after which he had not slept at all well.

Emily greeted him in the parlor while her mother seated herself quietly in the background, needlepoint in hand.

He executed a courtly bow to both women, then addressed himself to Emily. "I trust you are recovered from last night?"

"Yes, thank you."

He glanced toward the older woman in the corner, then back to Emily. What he had to ask, he wished to ask in private. "Perhaps we might walk in the garden," he suggested.

She nodded. A few moments later they were strolling down a gravel path among the primroses. Neither talked. But then, Emily rarely spoke unless spoken to. Would it be like that throughout their marriage? the earl wondered. His fingers closed over the ring box in his pocket.

He rounded a corner without taking the box out of his pocket. Once he proposed to Emily, he would have to marry her. Only a woman could cry off from an engagement. He suspected Emily would never do such a thing. It would create too much gossip for her taste.

Again they circled the garden. By now the silence had lengthened until he felt uncomfortable. If she felt it as well, however, she gave no sign.

He could keep a mistress after they were married, the earl consoled himself. He would find someone lively enough to compensate for the fact his intended bride was prim.

They were on their third trip about the garden before his fingers slid off the box. It fell back to its resting place in his pocket.

Whom was he kidding? He didn't want to have to keep a mistress. He wanted to be happy enough in his marriage that he did not look elsewhere for companionship. A month ago he might have been able to marry Emily, but something—well, something was different now.

With more haste than decorum, he escorted her back to her mother, bade farewell and escaped to his high-perch phaeton. Feeling like a man reprieved, he gathered up the reins and set off at a smart pace.

It wasn't until he was almost back to his house that it occurred to him he must begin his quest for a wife anew. There were many beautiful young women to choose from, yet he felt no enthusiasm for the task. Maybe he would wait until next year, or the year after. But what of the need for an heir? an insistent voice inside asked.

Turning the horses suddenly, he started for White's. A drink and some play might be what he needed to lift his spirits.

At White's he found his friend Lord Hertford sipping fine Irish whiskey. Lord Knole joined the marquis, and ordered a large glass of the same.

They found comfortable, worn chairs beside a fading fire and talked about estates and horseflesh until the whiskey began to make them more candid.

"The betting runs heavily here that you mean to marry Emily Simpson," the marquis observed, idly swirling the liquor in his crystal glass.

"Don't lay blunt on it."

"Already have."

By the fourth glass of whiskey, the earl was feeling mellow enough to confide, "I need an heir, James."

His companion yawned and stretched out long legs. "A problem we all must face sooner or later. It's what makes the Emily Simpsons of the world eminently practical."

"Hmmm."

"If it were me looking to get myself legshackled, I'd try for that pretty baggage you call your ward."

That sobered the earl somewhat. "Out of the question," he said more sharply than he had intended.

"She doesn't seem to be out of the question for half the nobility in London. Men with weightier titles than your own, I might add." Lord Hertford reached for the decanter to refill the sinking liquor in his glass.

Those men didn't know the truth of her birth, the earl reflected hazily. Yet it occurred to him that some important men had married women who had no social standing. They had married for the least rational of all reasons—because they were in love.

Which, of course, the earl was not. Still, he might send Priscilla a little gift just to show that . . . Well, just to be friendly. Flowers? No, she had flowers aplenty. Something out of the ordinary. He struggled to think of something. Then it dawned on him.

131

A piece of art. She liked to paint, didn't she? She was sure to appreciate a fine painting. He would send her one.

Perhaps he had acted improperly toward her last night by insisting on a dance. This would be a way of mending things between them.

Sitting on the bed in her room, Priscilla unwrapped the large, flat package that had been delivered a few moments earlier. As the brown wrapping paper fell away, she saw a framed painting of a Turner. Or at least a copy of a Turner. It was one of the first pieces she had given Geoffrey.

With nerveless fingers, she picked up the note that had arrived with the package. The scrawling masculine script read, "Thought you might enjoy this. Your servant, Lord Knole."

A chill ran over her. The earl knew.

Rising, she backed away from the picture, as if by distancing herself from it, she could make it go away. Yet it remained there on the bed, clear evidence of her unknowing complicity in Geoffrey's scheme.

She longed to confront Geoffrey, but he remained stubbornly absent. She had written him several notes asking him to call on her, but he had not replied.

If she could talk to him, perhaps he would go to the earl and explain it was all his doing. Surely she could prevail upon his nobler instincts to clear her name. She was willing to give him money, if that was what he wished.

She pivoted guiltily at the sound of a jaunty knock on the door. Mrs. Speers breezed in. "Good morning, pet. I heard you had a gift. Oh, there it is. What a lovely picture!"

"It's from Lord Knole," she said flatly.

"Such a dear man."

No, he was not. He was cruel. That he would send her this picture showed the depth of his disregard, even contempt, for her feelings. Now that the shock of receiving the picture was subsiding, she felt anguished that the earl would try to hurt her.

"Well," the older woman continued briskly, "we must decide what you are to wear tonight. The Courtney's parties are small, but *all* the right people will be there." She opened the doors of the wardrobe. "This cream sarcenet, I think. Don't you agree?"

"It's fine," Priscilla said numbly. Her gaze remained on the picture. What did the earl intend to do now? Was he going to expose her before all of London?

"You look as if you could use some rest, pet, before tonight. You're looking rather pale."

Once Mrs. Speers was gone, Priscilla hid the painting in the back of the closet. She did not fully understand what the earl was trying to tell her by his gift, but she did know she could not face him that evening. It had never been her habit to avoid unpleasantness, but at this moment, she felt afraid and overwhelmed. She also felt racked with a more personal grief. She took to her bed.

When Maria arrived at six to begin preparations for the evening, Priscilla roused herself enough to mumble, "I'm not feeling well. Tell Mrs. Speers I shan't be attending the party."

The resulting turmoil was more than Priscilla had anticipated. Hartshorn was sent up. Shortly afterward Mrs. Speers arrived to feel Priscilla's cheeks with a clammy hand and to ask a number of personal questions about her time of the month.

After she departed, Priscilla heard a knock on the front door and the sound of the door opening. Sitting up, she strained to listen.

"I'm dreadfully sorry, milord, but the poor kitten is ill and won't be able to go this evening."

"Ill," he repeated sharply. "What's wrong?"

"I do not know. She seemed fine earlier. I cannot tell that she has a fever. She just doesn't feel well."

"I see."

Priscilla might have been imagining it, but she thought she detected genuine disappointment in the earl's voice. Then she remembered the painting he had sent, and her stomach clutched nervously.

The earl took his leave quickly. Once the house was quiet again, Priscilla crawled out of bed and penned another letter to Geoffrey begging him to come talk to her.

The next day she received word he had left town and would be gone for over a week.

A week! She could not survive that long in this awful limbo.

She wandered about her room anxiously, unable to paint or eat, refusing callers and avoiding the earl. Once when Maria came into the room, Priscilla was tempted to confide her troubles, but the maid seemed so distracted that she did not.

Instead, she called for the horses to be put to and started out to visit Lady Roseman. Priscilla had no intention of confiding her troubles, but she hoped seeing her ladyship would be the diversion she desperately needed.

Unfortunately, when she arrived at the Roseman's mansion, she was told Lady Roseman had retired to the country for the remainder of her lying-in.

Disappointed, she listlessly directed the driver

toward the shops, where she tried to pass the time looking at fripperies.

The earl arrived again the following day. When she sent word down that she was not feeling well, she heard his reply all the way up in her room.

"Miss Springton was seen out yesterday in the shops. Pray tell her I await her presence in the study." The tone of his voice made it clear that he would brook no argument.

A maid arrived at her door to deliver his message.

"I heard," Priscilla said wearily. Slowly, she arose from the chaise, changed into a sprigged muslin, and went downstairs. The earl was pacing when she entered the study.

He looked formidable moving about the room with great strides. The dark scowl on his brow and the snapping green of his eyes did nothing to dispel that impression.

"Sit down," he greeted her brusquely.

She obeyed. The matter could be avoided no longer, she realized unhappily. Very well, she might as well face it with valor. "Milord, if I might say a word," she began.

Whirling from the window, he glared at her. "What?"

There was no hint of encouragement in his tone. Drawing herself up with dignity, she continued, "There's no point in delaying this discussion any longer. I want to talk about the painting."

"It's a bit late to thank me," he said with harsh sarcasm. "I must own I was surprised not to receive any word of gratitude. When a man presents a gift, he expects an acknowledgment, at the very least."

She could only stare. Was he serious?

He glanced around the room. "Have you hung it?"

Priscilla looked him squarely in the eye. The gloves were off now. "No, I have destroyed it. I might add that a better man would have come straight out and said what was on his mind instead of sending me that picture."

He drew himself up rigidly. "I don't think we need discuss my gift further. You've made your sentiments quite clear." He stalked toward the door. Abruptly, he turned back. "I may as well tell you I have received a proposal of marriage for you from an eligible party. Sir Trevor Kingsford. Before I discuss with him the true circumstances of your birth, do you wish to accept him?"

Her anger with the earl almost prevented her from replying, but logic took over. The baronet was rich and had influence. If she were his wife, he could surely exercise enough influence to settle the affair of the forged pictures. The earl would be absolved of all responsibility for her—something he must dearly wish judging from his dark scowl.

"Yes, I will accept him," she said crisply.

"Very well. I shall speak with him." His words could have chipped ice from a block.

She stood for a long time after he left, letting her racing heart return to normal. Her problems were solved, she realized. Had the earl sent her the painting so that she would feel obliged to marry the first man who offered for her in order to get herself out of this coil? Possibly. She wished he had dealt more honestly with her and cared enough about her to talk to her and help her try to find a solution to the problem.

But clearly that was not in his character.

Well, she had agreed to marry the baronet, so she

would make the best of it. So why did she feel so desperately unhappy? It had been her purpose in coming to London to find a husband, and she had succeeded. Was she now going to go about town looking gloomy?

No.

Chin rising, she resolved to play the role of the bride-to-be to the hilt. She would not give the earl the satisfaction of seeing her unhappy.

To that end, she attended the rout that evening wearing her prettiest sky blue satin and her widest smile. She had pinched enough color into her cheeks to make herself look excited, and she laughed gaily throughout the dinner.

Lord Knole was seated down the table from her, but she was aware of his glances in her direction.

When the Chesterfield's oldest daughter sat down at the pianoforte and others began to dance, she audaciously crossed the room to where the earl stood with elderly Mr. Wixham.

She stopped directly in front of Lord Knole, smiling up at him. "I have saved a dance for you."

He regarded her stonily.

The older man nudged him. "Well, go on, Knole. If I had a young gel asking *me* to dance, I wouldn't just stand there dumb."

"You're right, of course." The earl's sarcasm was evident to her even if the older gentleman missed it. Lord Knole offered his arm, and they proceeded to the section of the large room where other couples waltzed. He drew her into his arms and held her just the right distance and with just the right pressure. Her dancing was far from perfect, but she had improved considerably since he had aided her in those first lessons. Now, however, her feet seemed to falter.

"One, two, three," he said.

"Yes, I know." The brashness that had carried her this far this evening deserted her. She was in his arms, and suddenly she was confused. Letting her smile die away, she lowered her lashes. She didn't want to like him. She had no reason to like him. Yet there was something between them—a *feeling*—that was stronger than she could explain away.

"It occurred to me that I really should write to your father before speaking to Sir Trevor," he said flatly. He avoided looking at her. "Your father may wish to meet the man before he gives his approval for a marriage."

"Yes." Priscilla was privately relieved to have more time before confronting the reality of marriage.

The dance ended, and he released her. For an instant, she allowed her gaze to find his. They regarded each other silently. If all had gone as her father had planned, it would have been the earl she would be marrying instead of the baronet. She and Lord Knole would have shared a home together, had children, and grown old in each other's company. Slowly, she stepped away from him. This time when she smiled it was not a bright, artificial smile. It was one full of bittersweetness and regret. And she thought he looked back at her almost wistfully.

Then someone else asked her to dance, and her chance to express any of those thoughts to the earl was lost forever.

Chapter 10

Without her painting to keep her occupied, Priscilla found herself with nothing to do. The morning after the ball, she made several unsuccessful attempts to write letters home. But she was too preoccupied to concentrate. All she could think about was that she must marry quickly before anyone found out what she had done. Once she was wed, her husband would be bound to protect her. Wouldn't he? But what if . . . All she seemed to do was worry.

Perhaps a walk to the lending library might distract her, she thought, and summoned Maria.

When the maid appeared, Priscilla saw that deep lines were etched around her eyes, and her face looked haggard. Even her posture no longer seemed as upright.

Priscilla stared at her. "You're ill!"

"No, I'm fine," she said quickly.

"You don't look it. You aren't getting enough rest. Or else the climate in England does not suit you."

"I feel well," the maid insisted, but she looked close to tears.

Priscilla was unconvinced, but she let the matter

drop for the moment. She was guiltily aware that she had spent very little time with her maid over the past few weeks. She would wait a bit, until Maria felt relaxed with her again, before pressing the matter.

So Priscilla forced herself to chat idly about the weather and parties she had attended, while Maria assisted her into a cream cotton gown and fetched her pelisse and bonnet.

"You don't have your easel set up," Maria observed when she returned. "You've not been painting?"

"No, I've been too busy," she lied.

"It's a pity. You always enjoyed it."

"I used to." Priscilla doubted she would ever again enjoy painting the way she had before she became entangled with Geoffrey. That was the least of what had changed. She still did not know what her future held, and she resolutely tried to avoid thinking about it. "I'm ready," she announced.

The two women set off together walking toward the lending library. They covered the first block in silence. Priscilla's mind was so full of thoughts of painting, Geoffrey, and Lord Knole that she didn't pay much attention to Maria.

In fact, she was unaware she was setting such a brisk pace until she realized the maid had fallen behind. Stopping, she turned and saw Maria leaning against a brick wall.

She rushed back and put a hand on Maria's arm. "What's wrong?"

"I'm tired."

Priscilla stood uncertainly. Could it be the climate that was having this wearing effect on Maria? In India, the maid had been as strong as a horse and could walk for miles without so much as a stitch in her side. Now she looked so exhausted Priscilla doubted she could make it back to the house. "Wait here. I'll go back and have the carriage sent."

Maria shook her head feebly. "That's not necessary."

"I'll determine what's necessary," Priscilla said sternly. "Don't move."

Guilt added speed to her steps as she headed back to the house. She had known for days that something was amiss with Maria, yet she had been so absorbed in her own problems that she had not bothered to investigate. Now she feared Maria might be seriously ill.

Pushing through the front door of the stables, Priscilla hurried up to the stablehand. "Ezra, I need the carriage put to immediately."

Without waiting for a reply, she ran to the house and found Mrs. Speers. In the flurry that followed, Maria was brought to the house and placed in a downstairs back parlor. She laid weakly on the sofa until the doctor arrived.

He was a tall, thin man with a receding hairline. While Priscilla sat tensely and Mrs. Speers fluttered about, he prodded and poked and asked questions of the listless Maria. At length, he rose from beside the sofa, called Priscilla and her chaperone outside the room, and said grimly, "Your maid is suffering from exhaustion. Exactly how much work do you demand of her?"

Priscilla blinked in astonishment. "Very little. I have another maid to help serve me now. Maria does far less than she did for me in India. If anything, I would have feared she was bored."

He snorted harshly. "Not from the looks of her."

"Then she must be doing something outside of her employment here." Priscilla thought of the time

141

she had tried to follow her maid. Had Maria been telling the truth about going out to see London, or had she gone out for some other purpose?

"Whatever it is, it is to cease immediately. Her health is in far too precarious a condition. She needs rest. Total rest. Is that understood?" He glared from one to the other.

"Yes, sir." Both women nodded dutifully.

"Good day, ladies." He took an abrupt leave.

"Dear me," Mrs. Speers said faintly. "He was quite rude to us."

Priscilla wrung her hands. "He only spoke bluntly out of concern for Maria."

"Yes, of course. Well," the older woman continued, "we must see that she has the very best care." After a moment's pause, she added, "I daresay the earl ought to be notified."

"I suppose he should," Priscilla agreed slowly. The thought of seeing Lord Knole aroused conflicting emotions. The memory of the painting he had sent to her twisted the knot in her stomach even tighter. This was not a man who cared anything about her. Yet even as she thought that, something inside her rebelled. There had been times when he looked at her with tenderness; she was sure she had not been wrong about that.

"I thought I would have an answer by now," the baronet said tersely.

Sir Trevor was riding beside Lord Knole through Hyde Park. The earl was mounted on a spirited bay, and the baronet rode a dappled horse.

The earl was evasive. "These things take time. I promise I shall send word 'round to you as soon as something definite is decided."

"I could offer for another girl and have an answer immediately, you know."

Lord Knole regarded him coolly. "If it's a speedy answer you require, I'm certain you could ask elsewhere and get a firm reply. But you have set your sights on a diamond of the first water. One, I might add, that other gentlemen show a serious interest in. When the prize is this great, I think a bit of patience would serve you well."

Listening to his own words, the earl could barely repress a cynical scowl. He was offering wisdom and advice like a man who believed in what he said. But if *he* were awaiting an answer to a proposal, he would be as impatient as the baronet.

When it came right down to it, the earl could have managed to have an answer for Sir Trevor. The truth of the matter was that he was stalling. He didn't want to have the question of Priscilla's future settled. Once she was promised to another, she would be forever beyond his grasp.

At that thought, the earl jerked the bridle so sharply, the horse jumped.

The other man was quick to notice. "I've never seen you before when you couldn't control your horseflesh, Knole. Is something wrong?"

"Nothing."

Everything. When Priscilla Springton had been offered to him by her father, he had not wanted her. But that had been weeks ago—before he had seen the flash in her eyes and felt the contagion of her smile. That had been before the thought of seeing her made his pulse quicken.

Then he had dismissed her as unsuitable. Was she not still equally unsuitable? Nothing had changed as far as her social status. Her father was still a nabob and her mother a baker's daughter.

But men of quality had been known to marry beneath their stations. . . . Some of them quite happily.

The two men reached a fork in the road. "I have several calls to pay," the baronet said brusquely. "You *will* let me know shortly, won't you?"

"Of course."

The earl turned his horse in the opposite direction. He felt a deepening sense of loss as he thought about giving Priscilla over to Sir Trevor as his wife. She might still be a nabob's daughter, but his feelings for her had changed. An ironic smile twisted at his lips as he reflected that her feelings toward him had also changed. After all, she had destroyed the gift he had sent her. That hardly boded well for his own prospects as a suitor.

No, he might as well resign himself to the fact she would never be his.

Priscilla recognized the earl's footsteps in the hall even before he spoke. She was sitting beside the sleeping Maria. Tossing aside her futile attempt at needlepoint, she rose. She met the earl just outside the door.

"I had a message that there was a problem with one of your servants," he said.

She ignored the stiffness of his bearing and the fact that he avoided her gaze. "It's my maid Maria. It's simply dreadful. The doctor said she's collapsed from exhaustion."

"There's no need to chafe your hands so. I'm certain she'll recover with enough rest."

Priscilla was not so easily persuaded. Hours of sitting beside Maria's bed had given her imagination time to conjure up the worst possible consequences. "What if she doesn't recover? What if she gets worse and dies?"

"She won't."

He looked so strong and capable, and he spoke with such conviction, that Priscilla longed to turn all her worries over to him. He would know what to do. He would take care of everything.

In her present state, she didn't stop to consider that he was also the man who had sent her one of her own paintings, which meant she could not look to him for support. All she knew was that he radiated the strength she needed at this moment, and she looked hopefully up to him. She wished he would look at her; he seemed almost intent on avoiding her gaze. "You really believe she'll recover?"

"Of course. But we must make certain she has proper care. I shall send one of my own servants over to sit with her."

Priscilla nodded, still gazing up at him, willing him to look at her.

Finally he did and something seemed to catch fire in his eyes. He took a long breath. "Priscilla, I—"

She waited.

Abruptly, he shook his head. "It doesn't signify." In a rougher voice, he continued, "How did your maid come to be in this state?"

"I cannot imagine. I have been so busy of late that I haven't paid much attention to what she does. I did see her going off in a hackney coach alone once." She hesitated, then confided, "I was following her the day you met me. The other day I discovered her asleep in a chair in my room." He was standing close enough that she could feel his breath on her cheek. They spoke low so as not to disturb

145

Maria, but their whispers lent an air of intimacy and urgency to the meeting.

"Have you spoken with the other servants about the hours and company she has been keeping?"

The question surprised her. "No, it didn't occur to me."

"Is Mrs. Speers home?"

Priscilla shook her head. "She has gone out for the afternoon."

"Leaving you upset and tending a sick maid," he said disapprovingly. "She should have known better. Looking after the maid should not be your job at all."

"I don't mind," she said quickly.

"I shall make arrangements to have a servant sent over." He bowed stiffly and started down the hall, leaving her alone. She wished she could think of a reason to call him back—any reason so that he would be beside her again.

Then she heard the front door closing and knew he was gone.

The rest of the day Priscilla thought about him and those moments together in the hall.

It was not until she was preparing for bed late that evening that it occurred to her she was acting like a love-struck calf. She had seen girls this Season who wore their hearts on their sleeves and who positively simpered when around the object of their affections. She had never thought she would behave as foolishly as any of them. Yet she had looked at the earl this afternoon with all the adoration and infatuation of the worst of those girls.

However, when she deliberately closed her mind to the earl, the other thought that came to mind was the prospect of marrying Sir Trevor. She had told the earl that she would, but as time passed, it grew harder instead of easier to picture herself as his wife. If only she had a real choice, she fretted, tossing from side to side on the bed. But she needed someone with influence to help her escape punishment for the paintings she had forged. There was really no alternative except to marry the baronet.

Lord Knole was in his study the following afternoon with his ledger books spread out before him when Geoffrey Speers was announced.

What the devil did the man want? In the little time the earl had spent with him, he had gained a singularly unfavorable impression. The earl had not even liked the idea of the man being around Priscilla, but since he was Mrs. Speers's nephew, there had been little the earl could do about his presence. "Show him in," he said.

The younger man sauntered into the paneled room and glanced around. The arrogance in his manner bordered on insulting.

"How may I serve you?" the earl asked shortly.

Geoffrey sat down, crossed one leg over the other, and made a leisurely examination of his fingernails before looking up. "It's more how *I* might serve you."

"And how is that?"

"It concerns your ward, Miss Springton."

"What about her?" He was careful not not show it, but he felt himself tensing at the sound of her name.

"Quite a talented artist, don't you agree?"

Lord Knole had the impression the insolent puppy was playing with him. He shrugged. "I've never paid any attention. I haven't a great deal of time today, I'm afraid. Pray tell me what it is you wish to discuss."

"Very well." With a languid sigh, Geoffrey settled back in the chair. "Miss Springton does not paint idly; she does it for a purpose. How shall I put this delicately?"

"Say it outright," the earl snapped.

"Very well. She makes copies of important paintings and sells them to galleries as originals."

The earl stared. Had this fool taken leave of his senses? "You must be mistaken, Mr. Speers. The child's father is enormously wealthy. She has more money than she could ever possibly spend. Why would she be reduced to making fake copies of paintings?"

Geoffrey lifted his hand in a gesture of bafflement at the vagaries of human nature. "That's the way some people are. Perhaps she likes the challenge of fooling the gallery owners."

It crossed the earl's mind to throw Speers out bodily. There would be a deal of satisfaction in seeing Geoffrey land in the dust outside the back door. But something stayed him. "Why are you telling me this?"

"The chit is under your protection. I assumed you would want to know."

Lord Knole's gaze remained riveted on his visitor. "I find it difficult to believe that is your only interest."

"Well, I thought it might be worth something to you if I were to keep what I know secret." Geoffrey smiled sweetly. "After all, Miss Springton is the toast of the town right now, but I daresay her star would fade fast enough if word of this got about."

At the moment the earl didn't know whether to kill Geoffrey Speers or Priscilla. If a word of this were true, and it must be or this jackanapes wouldn't be here demanding money for his silence, then what kind of person was she?

Geoffrey examined his fingernails again. "It's a pity, but I suspect this news would ruin her prospects for the sort of alliance you had hoped for."

After a taut silence, the earl demanded, "Exactly how much is your silence worth?" He was amazed that he was able to speak so calmly when he was thinking about running Geoffrey through with the ceremonial sword hanging on the wall behind over the fireplace.

"Well, I wouldn't want to appear greedy. . . ."

"Name your price," Lord Knole said coldly.

"Five thousand pounds."

The earl drummed his fingers on the edge of his desk. "And how would I know you wouldn't blackmail me for more once you had the money in hand?"

Geoffrey winced. "It hurts that you think so little of me. However, once she is married, it would not be your problem anymore, would it? If I were to ask for a bit of blunt now and then in the future, I would apply to the lady's husband."

The earl rose and gripped the desk tightly. "Kindly leave your direction. I shall speak with Miss Springton and contact you later."

He smirked. "I shall be pleased to hear from you. Pray do not wait overlong."

The earl could have killed Geoffrey Speers for his smirk alone, but he forced himself to remain standing rigidly at his desk until the blackguard had departed. Then he sank back into his chair and stared at the fine gold inlay design at the edge of his desk. Could this all be a mistake?

There was only one way to find out, and that was to talk with Priscilla herself—something he intended to do without delay.

Chapter 11

Priscilla listened quietly as Serina, the skinny kitchen maid, fidgeted in the chair opposite her in the parlor.

"I knew that she was up late at night, miss—she has the room next to me, you know—but I didn't see any harm in her keeping whatever hours she wished, so I never said nothing to nobody."

"How late?"

The maid looked cowed. "I can't say. The light was usually on when I fell asleep."

Priscilla sighed. In her hands she held a neat stack of hand-embroidered tea towels that she had found in Maria's room. It appeared Maria had been doing an enormous amount of this type of work late at night, straining her eyes to make the tiny stitches and losing much sleep in the bargain.

"Beggin' your pardon, miss, will that be all?"

"Yes, you may go, Serina."

The maid rose, dropped a hasty curtsy, and scampered from the room.

Priscilla unfolded one of the towels and looked sadly at the intricate stitching. It must have taken hours to complete this one piece alone. Why had she gone to such trouble? Surely not for the money; she was paid well enough.

Mrs. Speers bustled into the room. "Priscilla, you must get ready. We're expected at the Sinclairs in a short time, and then we simply have to do some shopping to replace those worn gloves and fans of yours. Tonight, you know, we are going to Vauxhall Gardens."

Priscilla nodded without enthusiasm and started from the room. On the way up the stairs she recalled how she had once dreaded meeting the British aristocracy. Now she was neither perturbed nor particularly eager at the thought.

What was far more significant was that she no longer thought about returning to India. She found it odd to reflect that she had once pined to be back there. Her life had changed in many ways.

Once she became the baronet's wife, it would change even further.

She was in her room selecting a gown to wear to the Sinclairs' when Esther entered.

"His lordship is here and wishes to see you."

Why did her heart race at the sound of his name? More and more frequently of late she found herself gazing off into space and thinking of nothing more than the turn of his smile or the masterly way he handled his horses.

"Miss, did you hear me?"

"Yes, tell him I shall be down shortly."

She took time to select a becoming dress of pale yellow muslin with a short trail. Then she checked her reflection in the cheval glass and pinched color into her cheeks. On the way down the steps, she bit at her lips to redden them. Without any effort at all, a sparkle had come into her eyes.

When she stepped into the parlor, she saw the

earl standing by the window. He turned at the sound of her entrance.

She smiled at him. "Good afternoon, milord."

His reply was little more than a grunt. "Sit down." He jerked his head in the direction of a chair.

Priscilla's smile died immediately. Something was very wrong. What was more, she did not think she wanted to know what it was. Her impulse was to flee the room.

The earl stepped in front of the fireplace, turned and faced her squarely. "Geoffrey Speers came to see me yesterday."

She waited, straining to listen over the thudding of her heart. It cut at her to see Lord Knole regard her with such a harsh chill in his eyes.

"He said you have made fake copies of paintings. Is that true?"

Priscilla wet her dry lips with the tip of her tongue. "Yes." Why was he asking what he already knew?

The silence seemed interminable before he said, "Have you nothing more to say for yourself?"

"I didn't mean any harm."

The angle of his jaw became even more unyielding. "You also sold them to art galleries."

"*I* didn't sell them. Geoffrey did."

His fist hit the brick fireplace behind him, and Priscilla jumped. "You fall in with a wastrel and think that that justifies any wrong that you do."

She was on the edge of her chair, her voice rising in frustration. "I didn't know he was selling them. I gave them to him."

"Those pictures were signed. You forged the artists' names on them."

152

She sprang out of her chair. "I did not! Geoffrey must have done that later."

He didn't seem to hear her. In a dangerously quiet voice, he asked, "Precisely what is your relationship with Geoffrey Speers?"

"He is Mrs. Speers's nephew and sometimes comes to visit her. I have not seen him of late, although I have asked him to come to see me."

One eyebrow went up.

"To discuss the paintings." She could tell her explanation confused rather than clarified the matter. "Why did he come to you?" she demanded.

The earl laughed sardonically. "To have me buy his silence, of course."

That brought Priscilla up short. "His silence? I don't understand."

"It's very simple, my dear," he drawled. "He will say nothing of your activities if I pay him."

Priscilla sank back into the chair. Had it come to this? She had done Geoffrey a favor, and now he meant to destroy her? Why? She had never been unkind to him.

With an effort she pulled herself up straight and looked directly at the earl. "I am asking you to believe I knew nothing of what happened. I copied the pictures Geoffrey brought to me. I did it solely because I like to paint and because he asked me to. But I never put signatures on any of them."

The earl's expression remained unaltered. Looking at him, Priscilla felt defeated. What was the use of trying to change his mind? He had never had a high opinion of her; he was scarcely likely to revise it upward now.

Mustering all her strength, she rose. As bad as things had become, she had to know if she still had a way out. "Will this influence my marriage prospects?"

"Sir Trevor will not marry you if there is a scandal," he said bluntly.

"I see." So all her parents' hopes were about to be dashed. They had left India for nought. Not only would she remain a spinster, but she would subject her parents to scorching humiliation. Even that paled when she confronted the thought that she might go to Newgate Gaol.

She could not bring herself to ask if he meant to hand her over to the authorities. The closest she could manage was, "What do you intend to do now?"

"I am not certain," he said tightly. He strode to the door. "You may be assured that you shall be hearing from me." He disappeared out the door.

Sheer determination carried Priscilla up the steps to her room. There she collapsed onto the bed. The tears came slowly, trailing down her cheeks like water seeping from an endless spring. She wiped them away with the back of her hand and wondered what was going to happen to her now.

Naturally, she did not go to the Sinclairs' or to Vauxhall Gardens that evening.

"You would have a lovely time, pet," Mrs. Speers tried vainly to persuade her. "You would love the fiddlers in cocked hats, and Madame Saqui will climb up into the sky on a slack-rope. Really, I am persuaded it would lift your spirits to go."

But of course, nothing could lift Priscilla's spirits. She lay on her bed, tense with worry, and waited to see what would happen. Every time she heard footsteps outside her door, she feared it was the authorities come to take her away. But always the footsteps passed and she was left in limbo and misery.

The balding man at the Burlington Arcade shop was deferential to the point of obsequiousness to the earl. "I have a superb Thomas Girtin I'd like to show you, milord."

"Thank you, but I'm more interested in the Turner." Lord Knole walked to the painting hanging near the rear of the art shop.

The dealer followed. "The Turner is also very nice. Well worth the price."

The earl looked closer. "Ever had anyone sell you forged paintings?"

"Oh no, milord, we're very selective."

"So you would know a real Turner on sight?"

The dealer hesitated. "I pride myself on being an expert. There is always a chance of a mistake of course, but it's highly unlikely."

The earl studied the painting. It really was masterfully done. Until now he had dismissed Priscilla's brushwork as nothing more than a pastime akin to needlework. A new respect was born as he studied the picture. She had a great deal of talent.

The dealer was bright with anticipation. "I could have it delivered today if you wish to purchase it."

The earl turned to him. "Whom did you buy it from?"

The shopkeeper hesitated. Clearly he did not wish to say. It was just as clear that he was not accustomed to telling earls to mind their own business. "I can't recall."

"But you would have it written down in your ledger book?"

Further hesitation.

Lord Knole sighed. "Let's make this simple. I am

155

far more interested in who sold this painting to you than I am in buying it. The painting, by the by, is not real," he added casually. "It's a very good copy."

The dealer paled.

"If you wish to have an expert appraise it, you may do so. But he will tell you what I have just told you. You see, I know the person who made this painting. What I do not know is who sold it to you."

"A-a copy," the man said weakly. "I spent hundreds of pounds on it. And you say it's a copy."

The earl pressed on. "Did you buy it from a lady or a gentlemen?"

"It can't be a copy. He said the artist had given it to him as a personal favor and—"

"He?" the earl queried sharply. "Geoffrey Speers?"

"Yes, that was his name." The balding dealer looked helplessly at the earl. "Surely I can recover my money."

"I would not be so certain. My enquiries thus far have led me to the conclusion that Mr. Speers is deeply into gambling, and his pockets are sorely to let. Tell me, was there a lady with him when he came into the shop?"

"A lady? No. He was alone." He seemed to come out of his fog of misery for a moment. "There was a lady once—a young lady—who came into the shop. She seemed shocked at seeing the picture here. She wanted to know where I had gotten it, too," he mused.

The earl pressed some money into his hands. It wouldn't cover the cost of the painting, but it was a start. "Thank you for your time."

Priscilla was sitting in a chair in her room staring morosely at the carpet when she heard a carriage stop out front.

She remained impassive when the front door opened a few moments later. Not until she heard a familiar voice booming in the hall did she look up.

"Papa?" she murmured.

Immediately she was on her feet. She ran down the stairs and flung herself into her mother's arms.

Her mother engulfed her in a hug. "It's wonderful to see you, too, child."

"Why is she crying?" her father asked the room at large.

By then Mrs. Speers had arrived, and servants were shuffling about holding bandboxes and awaiting instructions.

"She's overwrought at seeing you," Mrs. Speers explained.

Priscilla hugged her father. "Oh, Papa!"

He put her at arm's length and smiled fondly down at her. "Your mother and I decided to come to London ourselves and meet this fellow who wants to marry you."

Fresh tears sprang forward, and Priscilla folded herself back against his chest.

"You're certain nothing's wrong?" A note of worry had crept into her father's voice.

"Nothing at all," Mrs. Speers assured him. "She is overjoyed at the sight of you. Come along into the parlor and let's introduce ourselves properly."

"The house is smaller than I had pictured," Victor Springton noted.

Priscilla was too relieved to see her father to chide him for his lack of tact. Papa had a lot of money. For a brief moment hope flared that he would be able to save her from gaol. That hope died quickly. Since coming to London she had learned there was a great deal of difference between money and influence. Her father, she now knew, possessed no social consequence and no influence.

"It was a long drive," her mother was saying.

"Dear me, where are my manners?" Mrs. Speers rose and began to flutter about. "You must be tired. I shall have rooms made ready for you."

As her chaperone left the room, Priscilla's father turned to her. "So when can we meet your baronet? If you and the earl approve of him, I'm certain he is an excellent match. All that remains is to arrange the details of the wedding."

Priscilla stood mute, caught between a reluctance to dash his hopes and a feeling of wanting to unburden herself of her grief.

Grasping for a solution, she said in a rush, "Papa, have you ever thought we should return to India? I've missed it dreadfully. I think Maria has, too. Probably all the servants have. We could go back there and live the way we always have and, well, there's really no need for me to marry at all."

Her father's smile faded into a frown. "What are you saying, child?"

"Maybe England isn't the place for us. Maybe we belong back in India."

"Of course this is our place," Mrs. Springton put in firmly. "We are English. It was never our intention to live out the rest of our days in a foreign country. We wanted to come back home so that you could raise your children on your native soil."

"The baronet's children," Victor Springton added proudly.

Priscilla took a deep breath. "Upon reflection, I do not think I wish to marry him."

That roused cries of dismay from both her parents. No longer able to bear her secret alone, Priscilla gave up prevarication and blurted the tale of Geoffrey and her uncertain legal predicament.

When she was finished, her father stood thunderstruck. Her mother was pale.

Mrs. Springton wrung her hands. "What's to be done?"

"My daughter in gaol?" Victor Springton said faintly.

"It's not certain," Priscilla said. "If Geoffrey is paid enough money, perhaps he will confess to his actions and—"

"I shall kill him," her father decided, and started from the room.

Alarmed, Priscilla caught at his arm. "It will serve little purpose for both of us to end up in gaol, Papa. We must find another solution."

"What does the earl say is to be done?" her mother asked faintly.

"Yes, the earl," her father said hotly. "Why has he not done something on your behalf? *He* is the one who brought you up to London and who was responsible for your welfare."

Priscilla avoided her father's gaze.

Her father did not intend to let the matter go lightly. "I shall go speak to Knole this instant."

It was at this juncture when Mrs. Speers returned and announced brightly, "Rooms are being prepared."

Victor Springton glared at her. "I would not spend one night under this roof, madam. I am leaving and taking my daughter with me."

Mrs. Speers looked blankly from one distraught face to the next.

"Have Priscilla's maid summoned," her father dictated.

That gave the chaperone something solid to address herself to. "Maria is ill. She cannot be taken out." She turned her confused gaze to Priscilla. "What is wrong?"

"The paintings that I made for Geoffrey—"

"Don't talk to her, Priscilla. She is doubtless in league with the scoundrel." Addressing himself to the hapless Mrs. Speers, Victor Springton continued, "You, madam, have subjected my daughter to a life of pure misery. I am surprised the earl could have considered you fit for a position of this responsibility. Lord Knole has a deal of answering to do," he muttered. Still holding Priscilla close, he shepherded her from the room. "I shall send a carriage back for my daughter's maid. Have her ready to go. Be warned I shall call the constable if you attempt to hold her."

"As if I would try to keep anyone against her will," she sniffed.

"Mrs. Speers, I'm dreadfully sorry about this," Priscilla said. "You see—"

"Come along, child" her father interrupted with a searing look at the chaperone. He led his wife and daughter out the door and slammed it in Mrs. Speers's face.

As he trundled her down the steps, Priscilla insisted, "Papa, she didn't know. You should have let me explain to her how matters stood."

He was not listening. Self-righteous anger made him deaf to all persuasions.

Victor Springton bundled Priscilla into the carriage beside her mother and climbed in after crisply directing the driver to Lord Knole's house.

Priscilla sat anxiously forward on her seat. She did not relish the humiliation that was soon to befall her, but she saw no way of deflecting it. Her father was determined to speak to Lord Knole.

160

The earl would shortly make it clear that any problems she had were her own. Afterward, when her father was calmer, he would see that they really *had* to return to India now, or at least somewhere that she would be safe.

Chapter 12

The earl was in his study when he heard the commotion in the entry hall.

"I'll show myself in. You just point the way," a strident male voice said.

"If you would give me your name, I will announce you," his footman tried tactfully.

"Never mind that! Where is Knole?"

The earl opened the door to his study and saw Victor Springton, Mrs. Springton, and Priscilla. All three looked agitated. "It's all right," he told the flustered footman.

"There you are, Knole." Victor Springton advanced down the hall toward him, an unpleasant look on his face.

Priscilla followed, clutching at his arm. Mrs. Springton, looking faint, remained behind.

The earl frowned. What was Springton doing in London? And what in the devil was wrong?

"See here, Knole, what kind of man are you?" Victor Springton flung a hand in Priscilla's direction. "My daughter was here under your protection. It was your duty to see to it that she did not become embroiled with unsavory characters. You've done a deuced poor job of that." His hands came to rest on his hips in an attitude of belligerence.

"Am I to infer from this you are speaking about your daughter's paintings?" the earl asked stiffly.

Victor Springton all but spat. "You are to infer that I think you owe me an explanation for the low-handed way you have handled this affair."

Priscilla put a pacifying hand on her father's shoulder. "Papa, perhaps—"

"You were to find her a husband, not land her in trouble. I've half a mind to call you out!"

Lord Knole's glance went from Springton's angry, red-splotched face to Priscilla's. "As far as a husband is concerned, under the circumstances the baronet will not wish—"

"Backing off, is he? I shouldn't wonder. You've made my child look a fool."

"No one knows yet about the paintings," the earl interrupted with impatient anger. "If you would but listen, I have a solution."

Springton fell silent. Judging from the fierce red of his face, his silence was because anger constricted his throat rather than because he wished to listen.

The earl seized the opportunity to speak. "You have the right of it that the baronet will not wish to marry Priscilla now. However, I am willing to offer myself as a substitute."

Priscilla could scarcely believe her ears. Lord Knole was offering to marry her! She was so mortified she felt like sliding behind the heavy velvet draperies. It took her a moment to find her voice, then she managed to whisper, "No, I don't—"

Her father turned his wrath on her. "You stay out of this." Wheeling back toward the earl, he demanded, "What makes you think I even consider you acceptable as a son after the shameful way you have proceeded?"

The muscle flexing in the earl's cheeks suggested his anger was building to match that of the older man. "Mr. Springton, I would advise you to give serious consideration before declining my offer."

"You're scarcely doing a favor, you know. You owe it to her to marry her."

Priscilla put cold hands to her warm cheeks. This couldn't really be happening. Marrying the earl under these appalling circumstances was the last thing she wanted. "Papa, I would as soon return to India and marry no one."

Her father glared at her. "That is not one of the options." Turning back to the earl, he said brusquely, "I accept your offer for my daughter's hand."

The earl was as cool as ice. "Very well. I shall have my solicitor draw up the papers."

"Under the circumstances," Victor Springton continued, "the ceremony should proceed as quickly as possible. You could get a special license and be married within three days."

Priscilla directed a pleading gaze toward her father. "Papa, I don't want to marry him."

For the first time, the earl looked directly at her. A mixture of emotions showed in his eyes. Behind the anger, she thought she saw pain. Or maybe it was simply the play of light in the room or the distortion caused by her own vision blurring with the tears crowding into her eyes.

The earl addressed himself to her father, but his gaze never left her. "I am trying to make the best of the situation, but I cannot do it with a reluctant bride. If your daughter does not wish to marry me, then there's an end to it."

Victor Springton slammed a fist against his open palm. "See here, child, I won't stand for your stubbornness. You have someone willing to marry you. What more could you want?"

What more indeed? "I want someone who *wants* to marry me instead of someone who is trapped into it," she said with a flare of spirit.

Her father made a guttural sound of contempt. "Don't get all prideful on me. Your mother and I did not bring you across an ocean to see you end up on the shelf."

No, they did not, Priscilla thought wearily. The fright went out of her. What other choice did she have except to agree to the match? "Very well," she said, her voice devoid of expression, "I shall marry the earl." Without another word, she turned and walked down the hall to her mother.

But the day that had progressed miserably thus far was not destined to improve.

Priscilla was settled in a room in the earl's house, with her mother as careful chaperone in the room on one side and her father in the room on the other. Sitting in a side chair beside the window in the somber blue room, she pondered her fate with a sinking heart.

She would never be happy with the earl, and he would never forgive her for trapping him into this. While it had never been her intention to marry for love, it seemed a terrible thing to be hated by one's husband.

The door to her room opened and her mother looked in. She was fanning herself rapidly. "It's the most dreadful thing. You must come downstairs. We have just received word from Mrs. Speers that Maria has disappeared."

Priscilla rushed down to the elegant drawing

room. There her father was complaining to anyone who would listen that things had been very poorly handled indeed for a couple of green girls to run wild in London. Priscilla's mother wrung a lace handkerchief. The earl—the very last person in the world Priscilla wished to see—was firing questions at a messenger. When the messenger left, he turned to her.

"Do you have any idea where your maid may have gone?" he demanded.

She could not look him full in the face. "No. But she is ill; she can't have gone far."

"The Speers woman is holding the girl captive, I say," Mr. Springton declared. "I shall go over there myself and see to matters. I fancy I can straighten this out in short order."

"Mr. Springton, pray sit down and be silent." There was enough anger in the earl's words to drop even Springton into the nearest chair, where he continued to mutter but did not interfere further.

Lord Knole faced her again. "Now then, Priscilla, think hard."

She shook her head. "Maria was doing needlework for someone, but I do not know who employed her. Or even why she was doing it."

"She's paid a king's ransom," her father put in. "She should have been happy."

"It's hard to be happy in a strange country," Priscilla said.

"Perhaps she was trying to earn money for her passage back."

Priscilla forgot her own troubles at the thought that perhaps life had been so dreadful for Maria that she had worked herself sick in order to escape it. Guilt settled on her like a weight. She should have seen Maria's misery, but she had been too caught up in her own affairs.

"I shall send someone down to the docks to see if she talked to any of the ship's captains who are sailing for India," the earl said.

Priscilla nodded, impressed in spite of herself that he was taking charge so admirably.

"You need not trouble yourself. I shall go myself," Victor Springton announced, and stalked out of the room.

"I think I must go lie down," Mrs. Springton said faintly, and followed her husband out.

That left only Priscilla and the earl in the large drawing room. Suddenly conscious of that fact, she rose. "I shall go, too, and—"

"Sit down." His words did not sound unkind, only weary.

She sat and fixed her eyes on her hands folded in her lap.

He sighed heavily. "I do not know how things came to this pass. All I know is that two people on the verge of marrying each other ought to at least *like* each other."

"Yes," she agreed, her eyes still deliberately fixed on her hands. "Since it's clear we do not like each other, do you wish to cry off?"

He laughed softly. "No. And it's only clear that one person does not like the other," he continued regretfully.

That gave her pause. She slid a sideways look at him and saw that he appeared to be perfectly sincere. In fact, regret lined his voice.

"I like you well enough, Priscilla."

She was becoming progressively more perplexed at the turn of the conversation. "But you sent me the picture."

167

"The picture? I sent it as a gift. I was trying—" He broke off, a look of illumination in his eyes. "Oh, I see. It was one of your own pictures."

"Yes."

Speaking as much to himself as her, he continued, "That explains much of your attitude."

Priscilla ventured a fuller look up at him. "Then you truly did not know that it was one of mine?" If that were true, then he had sent the picture as a gift. That thought so confused her, she blushed and looked away.

"No."

"I didn't know about the paintings until Geoffrey came to me. By the by, three art dealers stand ready to identify him as the man who sold them the paintings. I told him as much yesterday, right after I notified the Bow Street Runners. He was making frantic plans to leave England when the Runners apprehended him. He will not be troubling you further."

"He'll go to gaol?"

"Like as not."

She was silent, before saying slowly, "In that case, I would not have to marry." As Priscilla looked at the earl, the fist that had been tightly curled inside her stomach seemed to slowly uncurl.

"It is hard to know if he has already told someone," the earl said philosophically. "No, I think you still need the protection of my name."

They sat without speaking, both looking into the other's eyes. She was trying valiantly to read in his eyes all the meanings that she hoped were there.

"As my wife, you would have a great deal of social consequence."

Even as she murmured her agreement, it oc-

168

curred to her she had never before seen his eyes such a compelling shade of green.

A smile tugged at the corners of his mouth. "Priscilla, if you continue to look at me like that, I am going to be forced to conclude that you are not entirely indifferent to me."

She groped for the proper words but could find none. Instead, she said what was in her heart. "I think of you all the time. And at times I've hoped that you felt some tenderness for me."

His smile came into full play. "This is much better. Why don't you move a bit closer and tell me how you feel about me?"

She was without coyness as she slid closer and smiled radiantly up at him. "I have come to hold you in great affection, milord."

He kissed her then—slowly and not altogether tenderly, but very thoroughly. She felt the heat of his embrace tickle the length of her spine and start windmills spinning in her head. When he drew back she was flushed and breathless.

"That was much more satisfying than my last kiss," he said huskily.

For good measure, he kissed her again.

Really, she should have protested when he kissed her a third time. Instead, however, she found herself curled up on his lap with her arms twined around his neck.

"When do you think we should wed?" he asked thickly.

She was prevented from replying when the outer door opened and she heard her father's voice. "If you were not happy here, Maria, you had only to apply to me. I would have given you the funds to go home. You did not have to ruin your health trying to make money to pay your way back."

Priscilla couldn't hear all the words of Maria's answer, but the maid sounded grateful. Her gaze still riveted on the earl, she murmured, "It would appear that all has worked out well, but Maria would have saved everyone a deal of grief if she had told me that she was unhappy."

The earl's chuckle came from low in his throat. "It seems a good many people have kept their true feelings to themselves these past weeks, Priscilla."

She barely had time to agree before she was swept into yet another kiss. In a moment, she would protest that this was most unseeming. In a moment . . .

TAF-61